AUSTRALIAN
SHORT STORIES

No 67

T0359509

This issue is dedicated to Uncle Jim Berg and Uncle Stan Grant

First published in 2021 by Pascoe Publishing Pty Ltd.
10 Anglers Drive, Gipsy Point, Vic 3891

Australian Short Stories ISBN 978 0947087-47-0

Printed in Australia by
McPherson's Printing, 76 Nelson St, Maryborough, Victoria 3465

Cover Art by Joy Brentwood
Design by Stephen Pascoe

Australian Short Stories is indexed in Auslit and available on-line
and CD Rom.

This project has been assisted by the Australian Government through the
Australia Council of the Arts, its arts funding and advisory body.

CONTENTS

Illustrations by Yolande Oakley 7, Ian Pascoe 29, Photo loaned by Alan Jackson 35, Robin Cowcher 53, Stephanie Mew 83.

EDITORIAL

When we began Australian Short Stories magazine in 1982 the aim was to provide readership for Australia's talented writers. The short story has always been popular in this country but outlets had dwindled and become very university focused. That was natural enough because if it wasn't for the universities there would have been almost no publishing opportunity.

We also wanted to encourage the new Aboriginal and Torres Strait Islander writers because the story was integral to our culture. There are nine in this issue.

There are cultural links all the way through this issue. Marie Munkara arrived as a writer of rare excellence with her first book, Every Sweet Thing. I thought it was one of the best and cheekiest Australian novels I had read. We sought out Marie in the early days of the mag but the same can be said for Merlinda Bobis.

Merlinda is one of the strongest setter of dramatic scenery we have and in this story she talks about the Broome pearling industry. Co-incidentally the diver she referred to was my editor's relation so we asked Rachel Bin Salleh to add her perception of that family. I hope you agree with us that Rachel is a welcome surprise for Australian literature

One of our favourite writers and people was Gillian Mears and we miss her very badly as a writer and friend. Claire Aman evokes Gillian's wild presence beautifully.

I was in Brewarrina with Brad Steadman and other elders discussing the country and fish traps and Brad kept talking about red country black country. It turns out he was writing about these two faces of his land and here it is.

While we were in Bre we went to see the Aboriginal students of the Clontarf Foundation who were studying at the school. Great young people, great school but just as I was about to leave a lady sidled up to me to tell me she wanted to write about her family. Well, why not, here it is.

During a torrid time this year Uncle Jim Berg sent me a special stone from his country so that it could look after me. I have the stone with me always. But it was his words that gave me most reassurance in my work and identity.

Jim writes very richly about his Gunditjamara country but we thought we would share two of his powerful message poems for the sake of country.

Tony Birch is a great Australian writer and I hope people new to his work will search out his novels. The same can be said for Julia Prendergast who we got to know through the pages of the magazine.

I first met Melissa Lucashenko at the Adelaide Writers Festival and her quiet strength was impressive. Her novels and stories are a real bridge for Australians looking for an embrace of Aboriginal life.

Roger Vickery has published with us for decades as has Graham Sheil. Graham is responsible for introducing me to the mountains of Irian Jaya where the story for my novel, Ruby Eyed Coucal, emerged. The arrival of the Indonesian police was my fault.

I was lucky to meet Leslie Thiele and find out about her writing ambition but at the Olive Pink Gardens in Alice Springs I came across Maureen O'Keefe and her extraordinary stories.

Finally, I don't know who wrote the Uluru Statement and I don't think we will know. I'm told it was written by several people but that is not how it reads. It is so beautifully modulated, so modest in its demand, so gracious in its intent. But Malcolm Turnbull knocked it back by lunchtime of the day of its release.

Malcolm seems a decent man but in trying to appease some hard head colleagues who slouch close to racial hatred he rejected the most beautiful and modest letter Australia has ever received.

Here it is for all to enjoy and contemplate. Not an angry word, not a bitter thought, just love of country. I think it will prove to be irresistible.

This is the last Aussie Shorts from us. 67 issues of wonderful story but we now want another person or institution to carry it forward. It's hard work but so rewarding in terms of friendships with great Australians. We will never forget you.

Lyn Harwood is responsible for a lot of that hard work but her aesthetic judgement was paramount. We read over 1200 stories to select the crop for each issue and that task was shared between us. Thank you.

Happy writing and reading Australia. Tell and hold our story.

Bruce Pascoe

TUWATAYINGA

by Marie Munkara

Tuwatayinga my Maningow[1] always had to have the last word. Most times it was 'I told you so' and 'that's what happens when you don't listen' but it was her snort of contempt and her evil cackle that said the most. Maningow was born in a time when there was no separation of people and land, there was no before or now or time or space. Things just Were. Then one day the balanda[2] "boat people" arrived without warning (or proper authorisation I might add), but we'd always been known for our kindness and we let them stay because there was enough of everything to share with these people even if they

[1] Grandmother
[2] White people

were balandas. And then they built a mission and tried to teach us things like loving each other and not stealing. But we were too polite to tell them we already knew about all that stuff, so we just nodded our heads and acted like a bunch of dumb shits and off they'd go looking really pleased with themselves to think up more stupid things for us to learn. And that, Maningow insisted was our undoing, that was where everything started to unravel. And old Maningow spoke about these things a lot, in fact she spoke about them all the time and my brothers would roll their eyes as if to say 'oh no, won't she ever shut up'. And then I started to speak about these things too and everyone would say 'Oh, you're just like her, mad as a two bob watch'.

And then one day I looked at Maningow and realised that she was different to what she'd been the day before and every day after that there seemed to be less and less of her, and I knew she was dying and the world was going to have a big hole in it after she'd gone and taken her stories with her. But Maningow had to have the last word as usual and dying didn't deter her one bit because the stories kept on coming. Even after we'd taken her spirit to Tangiyow to join the others her voice didn't stop, the only difference was that her voice was inside my head now. On and on the stories and her cackling and snorting went just like before, and she'd start up at the most annoying times too like when I was on the toilet or trying to read a book. And there's nothing like a voice from the other side to distract you is there.

And then one day without any warning Maningow's voice was silent, it was like she'd run out of things to say, which is hard to imagine. I waited and waited but there wasn't even a faint little whisper to put my mind at ease. And then I started to feel jealous because I thought she might have found someone else to talk to, but no, none of my brothers could hear her (thank god they said) or the rest of my family (are you feeling sick they said), it was like she'd vanished off the face of the earth. And then I began to feel really lonely without Maningow's voice inside my head so I'd find myself calling her name in the hopes that she'd answer me and everything would be back to normal. But Maningow had disappeared alright. And do you think anyone else cared about where Maningow had got to, no they didn't.

'Why don't you shut the fuck up' my mean brothers would say, 'she's gone and she's not coming back. Ever!' Oh ye of no frigging faith I'd think as I'd sit in Maningow's favourite spot in the garden to wait for her.

And then one night when my mum was drunker than I'd ever seen her before, she sat me down and said that my constant worrying about Maningow was turning her and Dad into alcoholics and that if I didn't move out they would. Which I thought was pretty strange but if they wanted to leave the home that they'd seen all their kids grow up in, but then I guess it was up to them. By this time my brothers had already gone so I had the place all to myself after that. But you know how it is and after a while I started to get lonely and I tried ringing mum but I must have forgotten her number or something so after I rang aunty and got the right one, I found a razor blade and cut it into my arm so I wouldn't forget again. And it felt so good that I cut Maningow's name in the other arm but it came out a bit wonky because I can't write very well with my right hand. But when I rang the number it was disconnected so then I made all the numbers into eights because that's my lucky number. But when I was cutting more eights into my legs I must have pressed a bit hard because all of a sudden there was blood everywhere so off to the hospital I went and it was while I was getting stitched and bandaged up that I heard Maningow.

'Frigging hell she's back' I said to the doctor, 'she's come back!'

'Who?' the dopey woman asked, 'who's back?'

'My Maningow' I said, 'can't you hear her talking, she hasn't shut up for the past five minutes.' Well didn't that cause a stir because next thing there were two more doctors hovering around.

'Oh yes I can hear her' said the ugly one with piggy eyes. But I knew he was lying because he kept looking sideways at the other two who kept looking sideways at each other.

'How can you hear her when she isn't talking?' I said even though she really was. I wanted to see if they were making it up.

'Oh no I mean before when she was talking' he said.

'Well what was she saying' I asked. That's when the third one with the big arse told me they were going to have to give me a needle to calm me down.

'Oh great' I said, 'can I have two. I want them in my bum.'

And that's all there was until I woke up in a strange place with one hell of a headache and Maningow nattering away about the best way to gut fish. But I didn't like this place back then because everyone was really weird and if it hadn't been for the likes of people like Christopher who gave me these really great pills twice a day, I think I'd have gone crazy. But I do now, like this place I mean. So anyway one morning when I'd taken my pills and I was watching the lady in the seat next to me climb up the wall and across the ceiling like a big fat spider it suddenly occurred to me that maybe I'd gotten it all wrong, maybe just maybe Maningow hadn't left me at all and she was just testing to see how much I really loved her. And then I started crying because I just couldn't believe that she had ever doubted me, but then I couldn't stop laughing because it was the sort of crazy thing that she'd do. And I felt so good I wanted to jump off the roof and fly but Christopher gave me a needle so I could float around the room instead because it was raining outside.

So now dear old Tuwatayinga my Maningow who was born in a time when there was no separation of people and land and who died in a time when the land and the people had been irrevocably separated, is right here with me. And the space between us is filled with her words and our love and everything is just how it was before.

MY TENDER TENDER

by Merlinda Bobis

This is gospel.
— Uncle Freddy Corpus

'I was born wrapped in a web. Old folks say you'll never die in the sea
if you're born in a web. This is gospel.'

His tone is sure, his smile, disarming. Nenita's more than disarmed.
She's charmed to the bones as she shakes the hand of 91-year-old Fred
Corpus, one of Broome's and Darwin's last remaining hard-hat pearl
divers. She and her husband Arvis are all smiles in this corner of The
Roey. They're basking in Uncle Freddy, sunset-bright in his Hawaiian
shirt and with a very cold beer in hand. 'Smothered in ice, the only
way to drink beer.'

She laughs. 'You sound like James Bond! "Shaken, not stirred" —
the only way to drink martini.'

As tickled by Uncle Freddy's wit, Arvis offers to buy him another
beer.

'No, thanks,' he declines with a gracious smile. 'I like to get my
own.'

She hears her father's fierce declaration of independence. She sees
him in Uncle Freddy's combed back white hair, all spruced up for an
outing, and in the cane slung discreetly on his arm. It clunks as he
opens his wallet to show them a photo of young Freddy kitted up in
heavy diving suit, without helmet yet but roped and ready on a lugger,
its mast open and the ocean waiting behind him.

It all began a few minutes earlier. They were admiring the same
photo, blown-up on the wall at the back of the bar. Man ready to
take on the depths, waters waiting to take on the man. It will be a
matter of life and death. But bursting with vitality and young life, only
life, Freddy gleams under the sun. There are highlights on his brow,
nose, cheeks, and on his suit and boots. As if he were polished for
this adventure. The Western Australian Museum labels the photo thus:

'Aboriginal hard-hat diver Fred Corpus was considered as good as the Japanese divers.' As she stared at the handsome, young man on the wall, she couldn't help but see the young Filipinos in her first home. They made her heart go pit-a-pat when she was younger.

'That man — he's there.' A woman's voice behind them. French? They turn around. Yes, one of the barmaids, a backpacker from France, is pointing to the famous pearl diver drinking his beer. 'That's him!'

And so they're here at the bar. The manager sidles over, checks out Uncle Freddy's beer. 'That okay?' Uncle Freddy nods. 'I asked them to make sure your beer is okay and ready,' the manager says, gesturing towards the back room of the bar. Of course, smothered in ice.

Uncle Freddy rests his beer and opens his wallet to show them the same photo on the wall. A mini version, contained like an identity card. But Fred Corpus' history cannot be contained. It has crossed oceans and continents. He tells her that his grandfather Severo Corpus was a Filipino pearl diver from Manila who came to Broome in the late 1880s and married local Yawuru woman Maria Emma Ngobing. Grandfather Severo was among the so-named "Manilamen", the early Filipino migrant workers who tried their diving luck far away from home.

She's delighted by the connection. They introduce themselves and she tells him she's originally from the Philippines, then asks, 'Have you been there?'

He knows nothing of his grandfather's roots or home, so no, he's never visited. 'Look at *Forty Fathoms Deep*. The story of my grandfather is there, blackbird days.' Blackbirding of Aboriginal pearl divers was slavery in the 1800s.

She's all ears, tropics-sweaty and leaning against the bar sans drink because they've had one with lunch and were about to leave. But not now. They're entranced by story after story that takes her home. On the wall behind Uncle Freddy, a poster on the wall says, 'Sunday Family Funday' in bright red and blue, and where she's leaning, the wood is cool to the touch.

'My father was also a pearl diver, Achil Bin Salleh, a Javanese, and my Yawuru mother is Esther Corpus, they couldn't marry because of the law then.' Later, she'll learn about this law, the outlawing of their cross-racial marriage. 'I married Nancy Koolinda. Koolinda is the name of a boat, she was born in a boat. This is gospel.' His voice is conspiratorial, his gesture, certain. There's a flash of his gold and diamond ring, and a tug in her heart. He's like her storytelling father conspiring with his listener and he never ever forgot to slip on his gold ring, a gift from a brother-in-law, before he went for an outing.

'Look at this,' Uncle Freddy invites them to look closer. With one thumb, he covers the photo at the waist, and with the other, covers the knees, thus framing a section of his diving suit. 'See: it's a face.' Yes, she sees it! A face with a broad brow, its shadowed eyes looking downwards, and there's the nose too.

'I think it's the devil,' and he laughs. 'But the priest in Darwin said, "It's your guardian angel".' He adds that at the feet of his diver father's photo, there's also a face. 'This is gospel.'

It's a declaration of certainty. Believe me, I'm telling you the truth. And she readily believes because his storytelling is so familiar. It takes her back to her first home, not so much to her Catholic upbringing in the Philippines but to its indigenous beliefs before Catholic Spain arrived with the cross and the sword. Uncle Freddy takes her back to the other world and the uncanny, like strange faces appearing in photos. And guarding us, keeping us safe.

'How did you feel on your very first dive?' she asks.

'I was excited, I enjoyed it.'

'It was a matter of life and death … '

'Yes, but I had a very good tender, Ali Laka, 40 or 45 years old. He was very careful, he looked after me.'

Tender Ali Laka keeping Freddy Corpus safe.

She read before that the "at-tender" of a pearl diver is the one who manages the lifeline rope tied around his waist and the pump and hose from where he breathes precious air while diving into the deep. But the line goes deeper for her: it's the tenderness of an elder safeguarding the life of a boy. She can't tell Uncle Freddy this. He might find it too soft a thought about a dangerous feat of hardy men. But the thought is insistent, followed by a little niggle: for suspicious bigots these days, names like Ali Laka or Achil Bin Salleh may inspire fear, even hate. Hey, you look, sound and dress different, maybe you're Muslim, maybe you're dangerous.

Whatever happened to *tender Ali*? Like a rope, the phrase tugs at her heart and she's quickly connected to Ali's lifeline. No, it's not just her. We all must be connected, duly life-linked. It's the rope to trust: tenderness to make us kinder, kindness to keep us safe. Not quite gospel, more like a bid for trust. And young Freddy had plenty of it in his diving days.

The bar lights beam down on him like a benediction.

'Knowing I'd never die at sea, I undid the lifeline tied around me and gave three tugs on the rope. It means an emergency. So Ali pulled me up in a hurry — and I wasn't there!' But clever Freddy rode up to the surface on the air hose between his legs. 'When I got up, Ali said, "Don't ever do that again." This is gospel.'

When you're born in the web, you'll never die at sea.

How to trust that web into which all of us are born, or are continuously woven into throughout our lives? Filipino with Australian, and Yawuru with Javanese with Japanese with French, and many more lives interwoven, sometimes by blood or by water, or sometimes by simply meeting and telling stories like this moment.

Once she facilitated a storytelling project between Aboriginal elders and Filipina migrants in Sydney. The women were complete strangers and understandably wary of each other. For three days, around the dining table they told stories about family. So much remembering. An Aboriginal elder and a Filipina discovered that they both have loved ones who got into drugs at a very young age. One died of an overdose, the other self-harmed throughout his life. She heard murmurs in a corner: how much they loved and lost, and continue to love. Then a hush, then softly, 'We're the same.' Later, an Aboriginal elder recounted the wailing of women and dogs when the children were taken from their mothers in her community. A Filipina followed with the story about how she was taken twice to 'a safe house that wasn't safe' and tortured during Marcos' time. Another hush around the table. The stories were sinking into their skin, threading them together. Then the Filipina opened her palm beside the Aboriginal elder's and said, surprised, 'Look, we're the same colour!' Everyone looked to see what she meant: that whatever is the colour of our skin, our palm is always lighter, same as everyone else. Then she took the elder's hand. By instinct, everyone did the same with the next person. Who knows how it started, but soon they were singing *Amazing Grace*. Some were crying. All of them woven into a web, duly life-linked.

They're in Uncle Freddy's web now. Linked by chance at The Roey, entrusted with his life stories. And what a very lucky life.

'Not just luck,' her husband notes. 'That was hard, dangerous work.'

'I ducked bullets during the war,' Uncle Freddy continues. When Japanese fighter planes attacked Broome, thirteen-year-old Freddy hid in the mangroves.

The mangroves of Roebuck Bay? Earlier they visited this sprawl of green on earth so red, then further up, the aqua ocean glinting all the way to the horizon and a sky so blue. It made her think of infinity. Suddenly an interjection on the thought: birdsong! And something brown, or was it grey, darted past. A few more notes, they held their breaths, then it was gone. 'Like the *mayas*, the sparrows in my mother's garden,' she whispered to her husband. No, it was probably a dusky gerygone, a mangrove bird. After a while, two bigger birds circled above. Lower and lower, and they got bigger and bigger. What grace and span of wing, what mesmeric power. Kites hunting, she found out later from Tim, a Bardi guest at their hotel. 'Take care of your pets, or else,' he warned.

'I dodged sharks,' Uncle Freddy tells them, 'and got the bends three or four times, but I recovered. That was before I learned staging.'

Mangroves to ocean, sky to water. They've to be quick on their toes as he takes them from place to place, and she's a bit lost now.

'The bends, decompression illness that could kill. So you've got to do staging as you go up,' he explains. 'To dive twenty fathoms, you have to do six stages, half hour at sixty feet, then double to one hour, you double as you go up, I learned from a Yankee book on staging, the Japanese divers just did one stage so many of them died, you can see in the cemetery, I taught a full-blood Australian how to dive … he died at Bard Creek.'

She nods, trying to rise to the surface too, pulled up from her "technical lost-ness" in the art of diving. But story by story, trust by trust, Uncle Freddy guides her through his stages of remembering. She basks in his animation: He is my tender. His voice is my rope, steady, always with a gospel-ring. I hold on to it and marvel at the ease with which he offers me, a stranger, so many lives in one breath.

Later, when they visit the Broome cemetery, they'll see them together: different names, different lives sleeping on the same bed of red earth.

'Thank you for your stories,' she says, and her husband echoes her thanks. 'You're very generous with them,' she adds, and he smiles and tells more: in 1943 he salvaged a Dutch plane wreck. 'I saved a white man, this is gospel,' he goes on. The news said two pearl divers saved him, one of them was Freddy. But these Aboriginal divers were not named. Then onto another adventure: 'I shot a croc, largest in Northern Territory, 6.2 metres, this is gospel ... the news said, "shot by a poacher".' And yet another: in 1952 Freddy and another Aboriginal diver Eddie Roe, both 25 years old, broke the record for the most haul of pearl shells. All of four tonnes 400-weight in three and a half days, which is less than a neap tide. 'This is gospel too.'

He tells story after story with a bid for trust. *This is gospel.* Perhaps to counter the listener's possible disbelief and thus the teller's invisibility? Believe us, hear us, see us: we're here, we have always been here on our land and water, and not just as stories of dispossession and loss — we are those too, but we are more.

She shifts against the cool wood of the bar, keenly aware that she came much later than all these lives he's telling them. She's not from Broome, not from Australia. She needs to listen, to learn. In that storytelling project that she facilitated, one Aboriginal elder told her rather sternly before the session began, 'First, you have to listen to our stories.' Then she took the Filipina group through a map of their land.

'I was diving in Broome, in Darwin,' Uncle Freddy explains. 'I live there now.' Over in Darwin, he was able to negotiate good pay for pearl diving.

She thinks of the self-assured Australian larrikin but he's a cut above this type. He's not just smarts and cheer. He's warmth, dignity and pride. He's lived his stories of survival, of success, long before she came.

She thinks of the kindness of the storyteller and the listener, the kindness of the mouth and the ear. One gifts a story, the other gifts back a trusting ear. Only then can story grow. And prosper. The trusting ear is fertile. In it, the story tendrils sprout, spread and tickle the mouth to speak it again to another trusting ear, and perhaps another. We speak, we see, we believe. Together.

Before Uncle Freddy now, she's a child again listening, believing. He takes another swig of his beer smothered in ice, and she sees her storytelling father taking a swig, with great pleasure. Both love their beer.

'So how long did you dive for?' her husband asks.

'I started in 1947 and finished in 1961.'

They hear more stories. He has sixteen children and many grandchildren, he takes care of himself, cooks his own food, does his own laundry. She guesses he's on his own now, as independent as ever. Yes, he likes to buy his own beer.

'You're very lucky,' she says, 'surviving all those dangers.'

He says they should come tomorrow and he'll bring his records.

She gets more forward, playful. 'You look very young at 91. So, uhm, do you have a girlfriend?' Ah, she should have bitten her tongue. She's sounding like a *pakialamerang Pilipina*: a nosey Filipina. She's worried she's gone too far.

Eyes twinkling, he whispers, 'Yes, she's from Nigeria, she's 40.'

Her husband laughs. 'A very lucky man indeed.'

'Come tomorrow, I'll bring her picture.'

As promised, they're back at The Roey. Uncle Freddy is surrounded by friends and admiring fans. She's a new fan. She and her husband keep their distance, they don't wish to intrude. The Roey is noisy and crowding up. It's the opening of the Shinju Matsuri, the Festival of the Pearl, and Mr Fred Corpus is its longstanding patron. Yearly he's come to the Festival since he left Broome for Darwin, and, each time, every day he's at The Roey sitting at the same spot. Uncle Freddy's corner: the right side of the long bar, where the light is warm and the wood cool and polished by countless bodies that have leant on it for years.

He sees them and makes a move to rise from his stool. He leans against his cane, unsteady at first, and again she sees her father. 'Go and help him, please,' she asks her husband. He does and from where she sits close to the pool table, she sees him offer to help with the satchel he's carrying and his beer. No, not the beer, just the satchel. She smiles. He's protective of his drink. Like her father.

They walk slowly towards her, and there's a lump in her throat. Uncle Freddy is wearing a silky, pale green polo shirt, like what her father used to wear on special occasions. He's looking even more dapper today.

He sits down and takes out various memorabilia from the satchel. He opens one: it's a copy of the marriage certificate of his Filipino grandfather Severo Corpus Felipe and Yawuru grandmother Maria Emma Ngobing. She's speechless, honoured to be shared this document, and, more so, touched by this gesture affirming their Philippine connection. Severo and Emma were married by the Spanish priest Father Nicholas Emo who, she later learned, facilitated the validation of the outlawed relationships between Manilamen and local Aboriginal women from late 1800 to 1900. When cross-racial love was criminalised.

They take time to look closely at history.

Then he shows them photos of his family: first, Grandfather Severo and Grandmother Emma against a fence and trees, most likely the backyard of their home. Then, almost sepia now, one of himself with his mother Esther, brothers Henry and Richard, and sister Elsie. Then, the older Elsie and her husband with Freddy. Then, two pictures of his girlfriend Maureen. And from a newspaper clipping, one of his whole clan: sixteen children with all the grandchildren. He lays them before her with affection, with pride.

'May I get you another beer, sir?' her husband asks.

This time, Uncle Freddy nods. They've been introduced to family.

'I need a beer too, please,' she says. It's getting busier in The Roey, and warmer. She should feel at home, this is the tropics. She clips up her hair. Her collar is sticky with sweat, so is her brow. But Uncle Freddy stays cool and fresh in his shiny pale green. He tells them about his first dive, how his diver father was with him and didn't want him to go down. The elder safeguarding the boy. He pulls out more history from his satchel. There's *The Canberra Times* from 1952: 'Two Aboriginal half-castes have exploded the myth about the superiority of Japanese pearl divers and earned themselves £250 in a week doing it.' It's about how they broke the record of pearl shells haul, but 'some months ago, a suggestion was made the Japanese divers should be employed in the Australian pearling industry because Malays and Australian half-castes were not as good.'

Then, a photocopied picture of young Freddy with another Aboriginal diver, both chests bare and burnished under the sun, with the label: 'Two fine specimens of mixed blood divers ... ' Smiling, Uncle Freddy points to the label, repeats it: 'Two fine specimens.' There's pride in his voice, perhaps a touch of vanity, and she remembers her father looking at his young pictures with her and her siblings, and beaming as they said, '*Guwapong-guwapo* — very handsome!'

She smiles with Uncle Freddy, and her father. But there's a niggling discomfort. "Half-castes", "mixed blood". Racial tags of that time. And "fine specimens", its colonial evocation. But who is she to judge his pleasure over this description? He knows where he stands and she's here to listen. As she looks at the photo, she wants to say to him,

'*Guwapong-guwapo*,' as they said to their father.

They return to the very first photo where all this storytelling began: young Freddy in diving suit on the lugger. 'Open to page 51,' he says, he knows exactly where he is, as they look for him in *Lustre*, a book she brought with her. Then more news clippings and Broome brochures with the same shot: he's everywhere.

'You're the poster boy of Australian pearl diving!' she exclaims.

He shrugs, smiles. Beside his iconic photo, he lays down a new one: another young man kitted out for the dive. Same lugger, same ocean, same light.

'My friend, Simeon Bin Said. He took this photo of me, and I took this photo of him that day,' he explains.

But it's only Uncle Freddy now. Fred Corpus. A living history. At 91.

They're about to leave. They take the final swig of their beers.

'My father,' she starts, then clears her throat. 'He died last year. At 91.'

Silence. What to say next.

'Thank you for all your stories, Mr Freddy.'

'Yes, thank you,' her husband adds.

Uncle Freddy nods at her with a smile.

Now, how to say this next —

You gifted me my father's life. You made him come alive. You remind me of my father. You remind me that my father is guarding me, keeping me safe.

But she does not say it.

'Is it okay to have a photo with you, sir?'

He nods, he's used to this.

'Please take our photo.' She hands her husband her iPad and crosses over to Uncle Freddy's side. 'Wait, I'll undo my clip.' She shakes her hair loose. 'There, that's better.'

He smiles again, knowingly.

Yes, I'm vain too, Uncle Freddy.

She wants to put her arm around him, but all she can manage is a palm against the arm of his green shirt. It's an awkward pose. She hopes he doesn't mind.

The photo is taken and they say their goodbyes.

They walk him back to his corner at the bar where he's encircled by friends and fans. They keep walking, and an earlier thought follows her to the door: Uncle Freddy is my tender. *My tender tender.*

As they walk out of The Roey, her eyes get blurry. Must be the blinding tropic sun and this heat that feels like home.

THE MALAY METHUSELAH

by Rachel Bin Salleh

Dad, can I learn to count?
You already know how to count.
No, in Malay.
Ask Grandad.
Sure.
Can you write it down, so I can remember?

Satu, dua, tiga, empat, lima, enam, tujuh, lapan, sembilan, sepuluh

I learned by rote. Repeating it over and over, until it became second nature. Just like makan, makan dulu, kabar, bagus, selamat tinggal ... alongside other words and phrases that, with time, I have forgotten but were part of the fabric of my life well before I could speak.

Grandad Achil came from Malay Borneo, somewhere. He boarded the *SS Minderoo* and steamed out of Singapore. He came for the pearls, and he arrived at a time when Australia practiced apartheid under the White Australia policy. *SS Minderoo* had been built for trade between Singapore, the northern ports of Western Australia as well as Fremantle and Geraldton.

The name on his identification papers, faded with age, was completed with a flourish of a fountain pen. This name was not the one that I came to know him by and other details are sparse: Grandad was employed as a Lascar (sailor or militiaman); nationality Malay; age thirty; height 5'3"; and he had a 'scar on right hand'. Two faded sepia photos, show a striking man, browned by the sun with high cheekbones, full lips, dark eyes and broad shoulders. Grandad wore his songkok in both pictures.

Somehow Grandad's journey brought him to Broome. He made a

living amongst the hustle and bustle of a pearling life. The pearling heydays were hard and ugly, no matter how much romance we add to the mix. There was no safety net for any of the 'Asiatics' or the Aboriginal population in general. They were all separated from the broader population by the never-ending minutiae of 'black and Asian' blood quantum and racist laws. There was a pecking order that governed all aspects of life. He was Malay and ended up with Granny Katie. Where he sat amongst polite society was pretty low, and where my dad, my brother and I grew up was even lower.

Granny Katie, or Mimmy or Mim as we called our grandmother, Dad's mum, was a traditional Yawuru woman, with ties to Karajarri Country. She was birthed under a jigal tree on Thangoo station, across the Ming-blue waters of Roebuck Bay, south of Broome. Granny spoke language and often sang my younger brother Daniel and me to sleep with old language songs and her all-time Western favourite was 'How much is that doggie in the window'. She sang that softly and scratched our backs until both of us drifted off. I remember the texture of the skin on her arms and hands. Wrinkled and soft like caramelised crepe paper, when you touched her, she felt like a bed of rose petals. When she hugged my brother and me, she smelt of talcum powder and her kisses were as if a butterfly landed on our cheek. We were loved deeply amongst the silence and the trauma.

Grandad had had a big life before he married Granny but by the time I came along his past was well and truly behind him. Granny and Grandad were married when they were both quite old and had to apply for permission to do so from the government. Asians (in the pearling industry) and Aboriginal and Torres Strait Islander peoples weren't allowed to marry who they wanted. They had limited freedoms and couldn't escape the indentured servitude in which they were kept. They were able to marry in Perth and returned to Broome to 'legally cohabit' as husband and wife. Grandad observed his Muslim faith and Granny observed her Catholic one. We grew up in a Muslim-Catholic household and my brother and I watched as religious ceremonies unfolded all year round. We didn't understand that this wasn't the norm for the majority of Australian households.

Granny applied for and was successful in obtaining her Certificate of Citizenship. She received it on the 18 March 1946 and was officially 'legal'. There were many rules, but *the* important ones were not to talk language, drink, gamble or have family visit. She chose to ignore most of them. Granny and Grandad ran a busy gambling house from home. Grandad drank, and decades later Dad told me that Grandad used to hit Granny. The weekends, he said, were hard as he grew up. The Common Gate –the gate outside of which most Aboriginal people had to be by dusk – wasn't too far from their home. Lots of people sang out as they passed by, waved and stopped under the mango trees for conversation, a laugh or a feed. Many of the old Mims (grannies) and Aunties would come over and have a cup of tea and talk with Granny.

Grandad Achil and Granny Katie lived in an old Broome house, on a large block, surrounded and shaded by old mango trees that were full of noisy cicadas at dusk and fruit bats at night, young boabs and a dilapidated chicken coop that Blackie, our old dog, slept in. When I was very little this was the closest thing to a cubby house for Daniel and me. Granny was a collector of cats and, by default, fleas, which lived permanently under our house. The house sat on concrete stumps, above the pindan dirt which absolutely nothing grew on. Rickety old jarrah floorboards squeaked as we walked on them and not one window frame had glass in it; there was no lattice and no flywire. Ancient shutters were propped open by chocks of old jarrah and enclosed verandahs that encompassed the house. All the living was done on these verandah spaces and the bedrooms in the middle of the house.

Our kitchen was basic, and my brother and I were bathed in an old concrete trough that paraded as the laundry. Just outside the kitchen sat a large water tank, that housed hundreds of green tree frogs. I remember finding one so big that I didn't stop screaming and Dad smashed it with a shovel. Our toilet was out in the back yard, and it was the hottest, smelliest outhouse, with the biggest hole in the ground. Mum and Dad had to stand outside the door whenever I went to the toilet because I was too terrified to be left alone. I remember sitting on the wooden bench and constantly singing out if they were still there. I spent a great deal of time sitting in fear of the spiders that inhabited the toilet. They were hairy and I hated them. Years later, the shire built my grandparents a new flushing toilet. It was the most beautiful thing I had ever seen.

I wouldn't know until decades later about Grandad's life before I was born. By the time Daniel and I came into Granny and Grandad's lives, they were *old*. My earliest childhood memories were shaped by my grandparents and that house. My earliest recollections were not necessarily memories but more of an awareness of what Grandad was. From the minute I was born, *I did not like him.* To say that I was terrified of him before I had conscious awareness was an understatement. I can remember my Grandad picking me up for a photo – I was toddling around and when he lifted me into his arms, I fought and screamed like a banshee to get away from him. *I simply couldn't stand him.*

Grandad probably lived a full life, and was able to do so much, but when I came to know him, this Malay Methuselah was a dark shell of his former self. His later years consisted of him sitting on his old hospital chair on the verandah, menacing Daniel and me, and whatever I could do to irritate him, I did. As far as I can remember, Grandad was abusive and mean, and had not one redeeming virtue. He sat on his chair, in his buttoned-up short-sleeve shirt, with his baggy boxers, and he just glared. It was as if he was ready to go out but didn't get around to putting his trousers on. Grandad menaced the air with one squinty black eye and his mouth turned down in permanent disapproval. For most of the day he would sit with both eyes closed and his head resting on the back of the chair, but Daniel and I knew he was listening. He was listening to everything and missed nothing. Even when he pretended he was hard of hearing, I knew. Some of the old Malay divers and a handful of the old people believed he had 'pouri pouri', a black Malay magic of sorts. He definitely and silently 'sang' the darkness out of his soul, whilst he sat there, and he pushed it out into the world.

Grandad, when he could, hit Daniel and me as we walked past him and would use his walking stick to trip us up or hit us on the shins. We learnt to give him a wider and wider berth. As I got older, I started to stand up to him and became bolder. It wasn't long before I learnt that I could rush past him, out of reach, on my lime-green toy motorbike and scream at the top of my lungs *specifically* at him. And I literally mean scream. If ever there was a cathartic experience, that was it. The only thing he could do was angrily shout back. I have no recollection of Grandad speaking in complete sentences or having a conversation. I am sure he did but I never listened. I knew if I stayed outside the danger zone I could safely humbug him. Grandad would grunt and lash out with his walking stick. That stick was just as mean and ugly as him.

As I got more confident and more arsey Daniel would look at me as if I was deranged. I graduated from screaming fly-bys, to cruising beyond his beating arc and spitting at him. I realised quickly that I wasn't any good at it, so I practised on him whenever I could. I think more spit ended up on me, than it did him. It was Daniel that taught me how to spit as well as how to whistle. I engaged in a sustained guerrilla campaign. It didn't take long for Granny to find out about her arsehole grandchild and attempt to discipline me. I realised that she was also old and could only shuffle, so I literally danced outside her reach as well, but attention was mostly on trying to piss Grandad off.

I had a penchant for using matches and setting things on fire. One day, when Mum and Dad were at work, and Granny and Grandad were looking after us, I dragged a large pile of newspapers outside. I set myself up near the water tank and hose and began work in earnest. I scrunched newspapers into balls and methodically added backyard building materials as well as flotsam and jetsam. I stood back to admire my handiwork – a fine tower of crap. I leaned over and lit it and can honestly say that that little social experiment went sideways. The flames reached heights that were bigger than the house and nearly set it on fire. It was like nothing I had seen before. It burnt ferociously and blackened the shutters. I managed to turn on the hose and put it out but I knew I was done for. I slunk back inside hoping that no one would notice my smouldering social experiment.

Granny had had enough of me by then but she couldn't catch me to take me out. One morning not long after that unsuccessful research with matches, Daniel came and told me that Granny had some lollies she wanted to give to me, and that I had to go to her. I got pretty excited because it wasn't often we got lollies or sweets. He warned me with a whisper, that Granny didn't have lollies; she was going to belt me instead. I didn't believe him and trounced off. I skipped up to Granny and asked her where my lollies were – I was excited. As quickly as she could, Granny grabbed my upper arm and held on. Needless to say, I received a fair belting. Granny may have been old, but she was determined. Whatever colour I was, Granny slapped it off me, and then proceeded to knock me into the following week. It did little to curb me being obnoxious to Grandad. I just became more shrewd about it.

Not long after this particular belting, and after Dad had his turn at disciplining me, I got it into my head that Daniel and I would smash my toy motor bike to kingdom come. One afternoon as Grandad sat on his chair, watching the setting sun through the mango trees, I set out with conviction, and Daniel watched on in horror. Outside the front entrance to the house (we didn't have a front door), at the bottom of the stairs, I used large rocks to smash my most beloved possession into its next life. Grandad was shouting at me but wasn't able to get off his chair. The louder he shouted, the more determined I became, until I stood over a hot mess of lime-green plastic. It truly felt like I had achieved something even if I didn't know exactly what it was. Grandad was incandescent with rage. I later received a belting from Dad, who told me that it would 'hurt him' more than it did me, and I stood there knowing that was crap. After what felt like an eternity, the belting stopped and I was made to apologise to Grandad. I did, but I knew I was going to get him back at some stage. An uncomfortable and short-lived peace fell over the house. I think Grandad was secretly pleased about the destruction of the toy motorbike as not long after this I stopped spitting on him.

Life continued on as normal. Grandad got older, Granny died and we moved out of our old-shuttered Broome house, into a new Homeswest house, that wasn't very far from the Meatworks. This was in a newer area, that years later would become the first stage of the ever-moving Broome Bronx boundary. We were officially Black, White and Asian trash.

Then Grandad died. He died in Derby at the old peoples' home, Numbala Nunga. When Grandad was alive, Mum used to threaten that she would put him in there, and Grandad would get very upset. In fairness to Mum, it was usually when Grandad had just crapped on the floor in the shower, and I could hear the banter from my bedroom. I did feel sorry for him. Grandad's body was brought back to Broome, and all the old Malays laid his body out and performed funeral rites. He was placed in our old house, on the verandah, and dressed with his sarong and clothes. His body was washed and oiled and incense was burnt around him and throughout the house. I remember thinking it smelt like the Catholic incense (I suspect it was) and to this day, it is the smell I most associate with death. The old Malays said prayers and it was all very solemn. Grandad was buried in the Muslim section of the cemetery, in the earth, facing Mecca. It was the simplest funeral. Just the weeds, the dusty hot earth and a few Muslim old men. They dug him back into the earth, and I remember the pindan being shovelled onto his body and over his shroud.

When Grandad died, it was the first time I heard that he had other children. I don't know where I had been those last few years, living in the same house as him, but that was BIG news to me. Mum and Dad did not ONCE mention that Grandad had other children. The only reason I knew, was Freddy (his son) came into the house to see Grandad and to pay his last respects. I can remember looking at Mum and Dad and having a moment of complete disassociation. I clearly remember thinking: *Who are these people? I don't even know them. Who DOESN'T tell anyone this shit?* And when I asked Dad about Freddy, he pretty much didn't tell me shit anyway. No one spoke of Grandad and Freddy or of their lives. I realised when I got older, that Freddy was an adult when Dad came along and was a man living his own life, and all this was assumed knowledge. It didn't help that no one articulated these previous lives.

I really wanted to meet this 'new' long lost relative. I was excited, as there was nothing better than family you haven't met, but that was as far as I ever got with knowing Freddy.

I only have this distant memory of a man in our house, looking like Grandad.

VASCO

by Claire Aman

Before I learnt the language of map-making, the word cadastre sounded like a timbre or a cadence. It was a momentous drum, a hollow rat a tat. Bone, fire, dirt, stone. Like a shout, a ring, a knock, a blow.

But when I learned maps, I discovered cadastre meant the legal boundary. There was no sound to it at all, only lines. The lines are normally black but I have a range of colours and hatchings to choose from. Anyone wanting a map just needs to tell me which features they want.

A map can show anything. It's possible to make maps of black cockatoo sightings, of cropland, of underground cobalts or silvers. I can show all the creeks and rivers, with the sea as a great green mass. Or I can plot cockatoos and creeks on a map together, adding minor roads and tracks. This was the sort of map my neighbour Vasco liked.

Help me remember something good, Vasco.

Well, she was a great traveller. On her first trip she drove south in her van for seventeen hundred kilometres while I looked after her garden cats and worked at my mapping. She was gone for months. She'd write every week asking for maps showing particular features. I'd send them rolled up in cardboard tubes to Poste Restante at the central western towns she was expecting to pass through. Sometimes the maps she wanted were hopelessly specific, such as an Australia-wide geographical representation of variances in butcherbird song, or the distribution of various shaped stones around Quandialla. I did what I could, inventing features which didn't exist on my data base. A certain stand of clouds in the Maude district that suggested rain, later. When she returned from her great southern trip she showed me she'd stitched all the maps together in a patchwork, sewing on leaves or feathers in some places and adding figure drawings in smears of red clay. She pulled it out in a roll from under the wooden sleeping platform in the back of her van and unfurled it like a coloured sail.

When I held it to my face it smelt like all Vasco's things – campfire smoke, fragrant oils, bitter herbs.

I seldom travelled far in those days. On week days I had my work, often having to meet with state mandarins or land barons about what map needed to be made. It might sound strange, but I don't have to go anywhere to make a map. Everything I need is in my computer's geographic information system. Others have done the exploring, they have surveyed the contours and named the rivers and ranges.

Contours are indispensable for showing the precise lay of land. If you want topography, ask for contours. Or if it's bathymetry, if you want to know how deep the seabed lies, contours will tell you. When I click to display contours on a map, the fine lines spread slowly en masse up my screen, from bottom to top. It reminds me of vipassana meditation, when awareness spreads like a flush through your whole body from the tip of your head to your feet and up again. Vasco would smile at that. Unlike cadastre, contour is nothing to do with territory. It's about slope and gully and the points of mountains. It's about curve, fold, the feel. Contour runs its hands over the land's surfaces. Cadastre binds it.

Before I learnt mapping I thought contours resembled thumbprints. But it turned out that a thumbprint is about a person's unassailable singularity while a contour is just the vertical dimension of land. This kind of geographical fact was disappointing to Vasco, a romantic. She feared for my imagination. But as I often reminded her, I had debts which forced me to stay at my mapping.

Although I didn't travel great distances we took many weekend trips together in her van, often taking the forest roads of the Great Dividing Range. Once when we were driving down a mountain her bonnet flew up. We screamed as the old van took the bends blind, the bonnet like a great sail, the wheel next to the edge. Afterwards, pouring shiraz, we laughed and laughed.

We used to be children, skinny, with our hair in bunches. I grew up a thousand miles away from her until, at twenty-nine, I settled in her home town on the floodplain. I brought my old childhood blanket with me, orange and black knitted squares like ploughed paddocks. I'd used it as a saddle blanket and it smelled of horses. When I showed it to Vasco she buried her face in it. She was a great horsewoman. The oatmeal I bought in calico bags might have come from those flat paddocks. I saved my empty bags for her so she could embroider them with cats and lines of poetry.

These days I travel. After I'd paid off my debts I bought a small utility truck. Before I left, I sticky-taped her letters from her first trip together in chronological order. Those letters used to arrive in fat yellow envelopes, instantly recognizable. There were poems, drawings, post-it notes and notebook pages with the sentences curling out in all directions. Tiny messages scrawled in the corners, there always being one more thing to say. Stuck together they made a tatty, coloured thing, which I rolled up and tucked into a calico bag, thinking I'd use it to navigate. When I spread it out on my bonnet I have to rest my arms on it so no pieces come adrift and blow away.

So Vasco, did your wheel really come off on the Moonbi Hill?

I'm trying to reach the places she described in her letters. I'm trying to run our lines over and over this country so the maps can still include us. I've had to devise new symbols to show the landscape features: old camps, fireplaces where bread was baked, muddy tracks. Where she emptied her bucket. Things dropped, a dollar, a pen, a lid. Cafes she liked, birds, mechanics who had an affectionate pat for the old van, the post offices where she posted my letters.

Almost too much for a map, and it will take a long time.

Despite the mapping difficulties, I'm well-equipped. My utility has a khaki canopy on the back. I like your setup, says an ancient farmer in a petrol station, and I know Vasco would have been jealous. I sleep on the tray in a swag, rolling the canopy sides down if I want. Like Vasco, I take a box of brown rice, mustard oil and dried beans, setting my beans to soak in the morning.

I like Vasco's slow old country. I enjoy the long-leaved eucalypts, black soil plains, silver and purple clouds, the swirl of budgerigars. One afternoon I waded into the fast water of a Murrumbidgee channel and anchored my heels in the mud. The current slipped around my fingers like wind. Once she would have swum across. She was the swimmer, not me. She would have liked those rough old river redgums, too. I prefer that country to the coastal valleys where the cold comes down early and it gets dark in a minute, oppressively. Sometimes I think I've found a tree she meant, and I draw it on my letter-map. I mark my route, leaving a stick arrow at a turn-off or a button from my shirt on a stump. I circle showgrounds in red and yellow. You can always camp in a showground. I wrote a letter on paperbark and stuck it in a fork where I saw a butcherbird. But it's not an ecological exploration, or anthropological. I have nothing to discover. It's not a search party either. Too late for that.

Vasco liked following tracks down to swimming holes and making a campfire. She was brave. She camped in the unconsolidated areas where there are no zones to permit or prohibit anything, where people have to use their own judgement about what is possible. Once there was a brown snake slipping between her feet as she sat at her camp table. They're deadly, Vasco! But mostly her van was like a big safe horse moving along the back roads or at rest in clearings. I know she was happy in those times.

What else, Vasco?

Vegetation is a commonly used mapping layer, although unreliable in areas where forest is being cleared. Saltbush, saltier than salt, makes me happy. I love the stoop and crouch of mallee country. But the sheoak was the tree for us. Droplets sparkling on the tips after the rain, and the silkiness of the old needles when you lie down. The first time we ever spoke was in the sheoak grove at the end of our street. There were only twelve young trees. There was a tiny bird that would also visit, which Vasco said was a weebill.

Our houses in Vasco's hometown were side by side. It was a bird street with lorikeets at morning and evening, and magpies, and butcherbirds. The houses were weatherboard with ferny verandas and mosquitoes. Even though my kitchen window looked into her lounge room, we still wrote notes to each other with all the things we meant to say. We thought we'd always been a pair of shy laughing sheoak girls but there'd been a mistake with the geography when we were born. We even looked like sheoaks, often complimenting each other on the elegant droop of our branchlets and our fine leaves.

There's a story behind every cadastre. Sometimes the shape is odd, a rhomboid, two blocks consolidated into one or a small block excised from a larger one. The old explorers went questing through hard country dreaming of boundaries. We drew our own territory, making our cadastral line out of hay twine and red wool and the twigs we picked from our hair, and from mud and sticks arranged into figures dancing at the sky. The lines were in our faces and hands, we carried them in our fingerprints and as pictures drawn on a fogged windscreen, photographed and posted in a fat envelope. The body is a sensor, an indicator, a symptom. It helps us know where - and when - we are. Without a body we would float without legal boundaries in the air, or in the sea where there is no cadastre. We'd be lost like a star, unknown to our loved ones.

A map can help. Let it fold itself, it will find its familiar creases. But a crumpling started. I noticed her messy handwriting and how she craned over her steering wheel. I helped her rearrange her house. There's a trick to everything. We used sofas and tables to make navigation routes so she could feel her way from lounge to bedroom. We ran a rope, round turn and two half hitches, out to her back garden.

She gripped it as if she was in a storm and it was the world that pitched and rattled. Once I found her under a loquat tree, overturned.

But this is not about that. I wanted to mention the cheek kiss she tried to teach me - mwah! - that I never mastered. Our faces would slip, I'd miss and it meant we always greeted each other with laughter. We danced any way we could. We sat back to back on her floor as we ate our brown rice with red onion steeped in golden mustard oil, praising the handsome vegetables but later we'd each be holding a bag of Twisties, yellow pollen on our lips, a glass of red wine in the other hand. Nobody else said my name the same way. My heart soars when I see you, she told me once.

We loved words. We'd open her dictionary. Duramen. Durance. Dwindle: to languish, waste away, to vanish.

In winter the battery in her van went flat. She started talking about going sailing, but I didn't want those conversations. When I was seventeen I went out in a sailboat with my sister. A westerly came streaming in, I felt it warm on my cheek. Sailors can be taken by surprise, too busy looking at their sails to see the weather pile up silent behind them. The main sail jammed in the mast and we couldn't pull it down. The sky went black and the land vanished. We went yawing sideways into the waves, hoping for nothing else but to reach shelter. Vasco knew I didn't want to hear about sailing. She knew how I felt about the wind. But still she kept raising it.

Once in wheat country a big willi willi raced over dust paddocks and crossed the road right in front of me. It was only red wind but I slammed on my brakes. The wind is so unpredictable. You can't see it. Weather maps have contours but like many people I only half-understand them. It's green land, white cloud, blue sea and black contours, but the lines are not about the shape of the wind. Sheoaks let the wind slip through their branchlets. The young sheoak I planted in my garden is six feet high now. When I hold a branch the leaves are warm and coarse, like a horse's mane.

Cadastre is a lonely sound. Everyone is gone. Rusty iron banging in the wind. Look, the southerlies have blown sand against the seaward side and it's half-buried. A tree has blown onto a bush cemetery fence and snapped the old wire. Cadastre is only a fine black line but I can't shake off the sound. In my camping utility I'm trying to reach places where cadastre is not a feature, but there is always something – a fencepost, a sagging gate, a mailbox.

You're not supposed to abandon your cadastre, but Vasco did.

Water doesn't have cadastre. Depth is the boundary. Most of what we know about depth is from soundings of the seafloor, but ninety per cent of the deep-sea bottom is uncharted. It's a terrible place to rest, believe me. I've thought about it often enough.

There is so much more to say. Years ago I wrote on a spray of turpentine leaves and gave it to her. She stuck it on her dashboard for her first trip. It was a miraculous, faded, brittle thing, liable to crumble in a breath. When she came home she stuck it to the window-frame in her bedroom. It eventually formed itself into the shape of a little boat with a spinnaker full of wind.

See, sheoak gal, Vasco said.

But I still said no to any sea voyage. I couldn't bring myself to wave my great friend off into a toss of foam-speckled water.

But Vasco, you understood the weather maps better than I did because in the autumn you chose a gusting southerly. You let it catch your cape of hair and raise it aloft like a spinnaker, and all alone, you sailed off the map.

STAR STORY

by Alan Jackson, Goodooga (Mooriwarri)

(interview with Lyn Harwood and Bruce Pascoe
Saturday 21 March 2020 at Blackett, NSW.)

It looks like the photo was taken in the thirties or forties. It was certainly taken in the Goodooga Hall.

Several men are dancing on a rough stage. You can see audience members in the background. Most are Aboriginal. The dancers certainly are, in the photo Alan showed us there are two other figures dancing and all four are painted up in traditional Aboriginal design. Each man has a different design and Alan's grandfather is one of the dancers.

It is an amazing photograph because in that district the first white invaders probably arrived in the early 1840's but say seventy years later middle aged men are still dancing in the ochres of their family design but for a racially mixed audience and inside a public hall.

This is a link to a fragile past but Aboriginal people cling to such fragility with a tenacity that over time adds more calcium to the fragile skeleton.

Alan is also adding flesh to those bones. From a difficult life to a defiant and ambitious middle age Alan is working with men and women of his people, the Mooriwarri, and adjacent clans to try and revive cultural practice and support the young to do the same.

He is doing this for his ancestors. His great grandmother was Annie Jackson, one of only two to survive the Hospital Creek massacre. Alan doesn't dwell on the massacre but wants it to be a known part of our history. Another elder from the Yuin and Maneroo clans worked for decades to find the site of the Brodribb River massacre which only his great grandfather survived. Once the site was found Uncle Max invited all the descendants of the survivor but remarkably, also invited the descendants of the perpetrators.

When those descendants spoke you could have heard a pin drop. The listening was respectful, but filled with sorrow and incredulity. That is how history works, not by denial but by acceptance.

Alan has become fascinated by the night sky and is trawling through the memories of his grandparents' stories of the stars. A book produced by the Lachlan Catchment Management Authority, The Wiradjuri Astronomy Project, has become his bible and because he is deeply Christian, he is trying to draw parallels between the two belief systems. He discusses these ideas at great length with immediate family and cousins. He spends hours sitting outside at night studying the night sky and has been particularly enthralled by the transition between night and day, that moment when a line appears to be drawn across the sky.

He is particularly interested in how the sky predicts weather patterns. His grandfather, Shilling Jackson was a rainmaker and Alan is concerned about Australia's water policies, the waste, the greed and the damage both cause.

He remembers his grandfather fondly. The old man studied the habits of bower birds because they were known to collect opals to decorate their bowers. As Alan says: Shilling always seemed to have money!

He is a great storyteller and was keen to tell me about the moment he saw the duck revealed in the stars. He knows that as Yuin, I have a special affiliation with black duck. During summer the duck is in the north western sky. Although hard to see at first, once seen it stays with you forever. In that regard it is very similar to the Dark Emu which crosses the tale of the western constellation, Scorpio.

Urim and Thummin are two other stories he ponders every evening and they are tied up with the story of the dolphin and the horse.

There is a lot to recover so Alan and his mates are constantly on the phone comparing ancestral stories and the observation of the stars. It is a process of personal cultural recovery and a deeply philosophical process. It is an admirable dedication to the spiritual world and in his late middle age Alan's life is full of rich contemplation.

RED AND BLACK

by Brad Steadman

A story of the black the red and the sky country,
the lie of the land the flow of the water as the lore of the land
from the creators' footprints to the progress footprint.

Acknowledgements
Mum, Dad, my sisters and brothers Granny Williams, Nan Knight,
Aunty Dot, Alma Grace Williams, Gladys Lawson, Eliza Kennedy,
Steve Shaw, Jack Murray, Big Boss of Crocodile Island, Big Bill
Neidje, David Mowajali and Geoffrey Lee

Our old people saw the world and its changes and then the next generation had to deal and understand the cataclysmic rate of that change. Our great grand parents and grandparents saw the industrialisation of food production and land clearing practices and the abuse of water resources by what I call mechanistic minds and how that ideology changed everything.

There were multi-layered events across generations of family and history. My great aunty told me that when she was a girl on the red flats around Byrock she was shown and told about significant sites by old JM. This one story she told: there was a big rain and small fish had fallen out of the sky.

The fish kill that happened recently in the Darling river at Menindee where two hundred and fifty thousand fish including many old cods, yellow belly, bony bream and, of course, carp makes me think of her story.

When explorers so called discovered the west and north west of what was to become NSW they saw different species of fish but also symbols of death, They also saw small, white egg shaped balls in and around the houses. The old people's language name for brain is the head egg. This might sound a strange combination of things to give some understanding of how we are in a mess in relation to water, but also in our ideology we are a mystery to ourselves.

My knowledge of these things is a culmination of many years of listening, learning, travelling, research, contemplation and returning home. I have met so many humble people, sadly now many have died, but their life was one of quiet contentment. If approached with humility interest and knowledge they opened up a world we only hear or read about. Life to them was not a burden but it had its trials and tribulations.

In research you have development, what I call a bullshit filter, a way of seeing through the misinterpretation, mistranslation, misinformation and missing of the point of what our old people were trying to get through to us.

The creation story of the river tells of how the creator speared a fish in the water hole called gooroongara, a black bream. He speared the fish but didn't kill it. He speared it again and still didn't kill it. The fish dived into the mud to escape the spears but the creator followed the fish through every twist and turn, trying to spear and kill it. The hunt continued for the full length of the river creating the stream we now call the Barwon Darling.

The second part of the story tells of when the creator was called back to help the people who were suffering in a great drought. The creator brought his sons and their dogs to design the fish trap which was laid out and constructed by the people. The creator also gave the people the songs and dances to call the rain , so they sang and danced until they were exhausted and collapsed

As they danced the dust rose into the air to make clouds and out of the cloud came the rain and out of the water rose the fish so everyone was fed and watered and all the people lived on. To leave his mark the creator left his footprint in the rock at Brewarrina.

The two sons separated. One went down river, the other went up river. The dogs went north. Their tracks became the tributaries that feed into the Barwon-Darling. Brewarrina and the fish traps are unique in another way. Brewarrina sits in the centre of five bio regions; the western edge of the Brigalow belt, the northern end of the Cobar peneplain, the southern end of the Gidgee and Mitchell grass belt, the western edge of the gibber plains and lastly in the centre of the Barwon/Darling riverine.

The earth with all its different colours, forms, and shapes is as old as the old and as new as the new, because it is an eternal process of change and re-forming. The red country of Australia is called the red heart. It is also said to be some of the oldest rock on earth and the black soil fits into the same geological period.

These countries around Brewarrina are made of many elements; vegetation, minerals, ores, and broken-down granite and trees and their debris. Some hold copper, gold, uranium, diamonds, opals and gases. The old people, moving across the land, were using and deliberately not using certain minerals but in the modern exploitation of these minerals and water it is important to understand that we are finite beings with finite resources.

The earth itself, whether we admit it or not, defined or confined by our law, is itself a being of lore despite our constant demands and interference.

So, does the red and black exist as two distinct types of country, mutually exclusive or as mutually inclusive? Well, that depends on the interplay of soils, trees, minerals, ores, gases and the essentials of wind, fire and most importantly water. The two soils can and do exist as defined and also intertwined, varying in space, between places. So, it depends on where, what, and how it happened in the landscape; how much wind, fire and water formed the land.

Along the Barwon, Darling and Murray rivers paddle steamers traded and the first boat to reach Brewarrina was the *Captain William Randall* in 1859. Their trade was hauling goods: wool, wood, dried fruit and livestock. In the 1880's there were as many as 173 paddle steamers carrying 30,000 tons of cargo between Euston, Mildura, Wentworth, Wilcannia, Bourke, Brewarrina and Walgett, to as far as Collarenebri. Among the fleet there were smaller paddle boats, *Brewarrina, The Cato*, and *The Wandering Jew* which burnt and sank at Brewarrina.

In one article Captain Randall said that, ' the blackfellows at Fort Bourke were terribly frightened by the noise of the vessel.' I was told as a kid an old story of my granny great grandmother. She said she threatened the older girls, who were sneaking out at night, that she would tell the Mission manager if they didn't take her to see the paddle steamers passing by.

There is also another story told by Doreen Wright about old King Clyde and the Waawai, a water spirit. The steamer was going down the river and as it came down to a big bend called the Mirriguna the boat paddles were spinning but the boat was not budging. Firstly, people thought it was stuck on a sand bar, then a stump or log. But 'no', Old King said, 'I know what it is. I'll dive in.'

The captain and the people waited for Old King. After a while, because he had not come up, they thought he had drowned. Then up popped the Old King, and as soon as he stepped foot on the boat again he said, 'We'll go now.' And the boat steamed off down the river.

The main point from the story is the Wawai had hold of the boat and because Old King was clever, he could talk to the Wawai. The old people's stories and beliefs were and still are helping us learn and understand about the river and ourselves.

The paddle steamers did help feed and sustain the people of the outback and yes, did help to expand the nation, so for me there is no point getting into a blame and guilt game or to reminisce and buy into the romance, but I do want to bring people's minds and hearts to understand the impact this had on the old people who lived and belonged there for thousands of years.

How much wood did it take to build one boat? How much wood did it take to fuel just one boat for one year, let alone 173 boats, or the impact on the river system of building multiple wharves, locks and canals.

Irrigation started on the Barwon Darling in the 1880s. In the first year, 10 megalitres were taken out but in the next year the whole summer flow of 1800 megalitres was extracted. And thus the beginning of the problems we are still living with today in managing the rivers or more appropriately, mismanaging.

The river flows through the red and the black, the water and land all of them nourish and sustain us but we are dying of thirst for physical water as we continue to dry the country out by our reckless behaviour. It is really the thirst for knowledge of how to live in this country we are seeking that is now more essential than ever. If we only take the time to learn we walk between two rivers the earthly and the celestial, the milky way, which we are meant to learn from and to live with. In a mutually nourishing and sustaining way we look after the water, land and sky and they look after us; it's reciprocal if only we learn to follow together. It is our imperative and our responsibility to learn how to do it now.

BREWARRINA

by Dianne Kelly

Today I am going down the river with my family.

My uncles and auntys the old elders of our mob know where we can go where we can set up our camp for the day.

Where the ground is flat for making a fire to cook. Like grilled sausages, johnny cakes and any fish we might catch. Put the billy on the red hot coals to make strong black tea for our elders because they love to drink strong black tea.

All of us mob are going to have a look around to see what we can find. Maybe we can find some bush tomatoes.

MY MESSAGE TO THE YOUNG KOORIS OF VICTORIA

by Jim Berg

Young Koories of this Land now called Australia.
You are the Custodians, Educators and Ambassadors
Of the
Oldest Continent and Resilient Culture in the World
Stand Tall
Maintain your
Culture, Language, Identity, Spirituality, Dignity and Pride
Be proud of who you are
May the Spirits of my Ancestors be with you on
Your Life Journeys

COASTAL DREAMING

by Jim Berg

At the mouth of the Hopkins River
As it flows into the sea
You will feel your feet sink into the wet sand
And sea shells under foot,
Sea weed and sand between your toes
Kelp from the depth of the ocean being swept up
And onto the beach.

Smell the sea as you walk along
The rocky shore and sandy dunes
Covered with sharp edged native grasses
And pigface plants under your feet.

And sitting on top of these sandy dunes
Is Kilarney Beach
Where you will find middens
Covered with sand and shells all round
Blackened fire-stones
Laying on the sand

Take a deep breath.
Inhale the smells of the sea, fire and smoke
The aroma of abalone, lobster, scallops and shell fish cooking in their
own juices,
On hot coals over the fires

Hear the laughter of the Elders, mothers and dads
And their children enjoying their tucker
That they harvest from the sea.

They are practising a Culture that they had
For thousands and thousands of years.

Can you imagine being there?

Keep standing on the sandy dunes with your eyes closed
And look towards the sea.

Can you also imagine seeing
White sails on the horizon
Where the sea meets the sky?

These sailing ships are carrying invaders
That will destroy this peaceful scene of happy smiling faces.

These invaders bring with them diseases, the common cold, smallpox
in blankets, rifles, bullets, bayonets, the sword, the bible

And Genocide

We were forced off our Land

Destruction of our Culture, Language, Identity, Spirituality, Dignity
and Pride and Stolen Generations They destroyed and wiped out
whole Koorie Nations.

Open your eyes
Can you imagine that this took place in this country
Now called Australia.

WITHOUT SIN

by Tony Birch

The incident occurred on the day of Jonah Webb's fortieth birthday. He walked from the river camp to town as he did each weekday and Saturday morning, to Bobby Chuck's garage where he worked as a roustabout and general helper. Jonah mixed with few people in the town beyond the nod of the head. The day he was born, the white man who'd fathered Jonah took one look at the new-born and disowned both him and his teenage mother.

'That kid has something wrong with him,' the baby's father had said, chasing any excuse to give up responsibility for Jonah. 'See the way his eyes are rolling around in his head. This kid isn't right. Must be retarded.'

The prognosis of a fly-by-night farm labourer was enough for Jonah to be put into the care of his Aboriginal grandmother, living at a river encampment with twenty or thirty extended family, depending on the time of year. Jonah loved the river and enjoyed the freedom of bush learning, free of the shackles of a school classroom. Whether his lack of formal education was a genuine cause, or it was due to the prejudice of the town, Jonah was labelled slow at a young age and suffered the taunts of bullies anytime he walked into town as a young teenager, searching for menial labouring work that could bring cash to the river camp mob.

No one knew for certain why Bobby Chuck took him on and paid him a whiteman's wage, cash-in-hand. A nasty rumour circulated the town that in exchange for providing work to Jonah, Bobby would occasionally bed the boy's grandmother in the washroom behind the garage. The story was baseless, and although most knew it to be so, the truth was no substitute for the necessary denigration of a strong Aboriginal woman. The closest story to the facts was that Bobby Chuck's own father has treated the river mob harshly across the years, robbing them over the price of machine oil and kerosene, while spouting words of such hatred that young Bobby became disgusted in his own father. Whatever the reason, Bobby and Jonah got along from day one on the job together. Twenty-five years later, almost to the day, when Jonah walked into the garage Bobby handed him a gift, wrapped in brown paper, tied together with string.

'Happy Birthday, Jonah. Forty years old. I'll have to retire soon and give you the keys to the shop.'

Jonah took the parcel and answered in a quiet voice, as he always did. 'Thank you, Bobby. That's kind of you.' He put the unopened parcel on the workbench.

'Hey,' Bobby said. 'Aren't you going to open it? You have to open your present, Jonah.'

'Not until I've done the tea,' Jonah said.

The day Jonah started work at the garage, Bobby told him that his first job of a morning would be to brew the tea. 'Put some steam in the boiler,' Bobby called it. Over the years, on many occasions, Bobby had told Jonah that the time had now come to share the duties. 'You're no longer my apprentice,' he said. 'You're a man now.'

Jonah was a man. But he wouldn't have the tea ritual taken away from him so easily. 'Sorry, Bobby,' he'd explained on more than one occasion. 'This is my job, not yours.'

'Come on,' Bobby insisted. 'It's your birthday. At least let me make the tea this morning.'

Jonah briefly considered the offer before rejecting it. 'It's been my birthday plenty of times before this morning, Bobby, and I made the tea on those days. I'll do it again this morning, if you don't mind.'

'But you're forty years old today,' Bobby said. 'This birthday is a special one.'

'So is making the tea,' Jonah insisted.

Bobby let the matter rest. He sat at the workbench and waited for his morning cup of tea, wearing his lifelong uniform of an oil-stained boiler-suit over one of Mrs Chuck's hand-knitted jumpers and a Castrol cap over his balding skull. He reached into his workbag, bought out a cake tin and placed it next to Jonah's birthday gift. The two men sat in the early light enjoying their tea and apple cake until Jonah eventually opened his gift, a finely crafted hunting knife presented in a leather pouch. He held the blade to the light. 'This is beautiful, Bobby. Thank you so much.'

'This knife,' Bobby said. 'Is the best you can get. You could skin a hundred rabbits a day, every day for the rest of your life, Jonah, and that blade will never go blunt on you.'

Jonah sat at the bench admiring the knife. Bobby tidied up and then smacked his hands together. 'We best start work. Or it will be lunchtime and we'll have nothing to show for our day.'

Each Friday Bobby Chuck left the garage around noon and completed his weekly business. He visited the post office, the bank and picked up the groceries for the weekend. He usually returned to the garage and worked for another hour or so before leaving Jonah to clean up and lock the garage around sunset, whatever the time of year. Bobby was at the bank and Jonah was sitting behind the counter when a sedan trailing black smoke pulled into the garage and parked beside the bowser. Ray Jeans sat behind the wheel, and a cousin, Kelvin, rode shotgun. A third man, unnamed and unknown to Jonah was sprawled across the back seat, drunk and asleep. Jonah wiped his hands on a cloth rag hanging from his overalls pocket and walked out to the car. Ray Jeans was trouble. Jonah nervously buried his hands deep in his pockets.

'You fellas after petrol?' he asked.

'No,' Ray snarled. 'I'm looking for a bag of onions.'

'Oh, we don't sell onions here,' Jonah said, remaining polite.

'No shit?' Ray said. His front seat companion leaned forward, crossed his eye mockingly and laughed at Jonah.

'No onions? We'll take some petrol then,' Ray said.

'How much?' Jonah asked.

'Fill the tank.'

Jonah stood at the bowser filling the car. Both Ray and Kelvin got out, stood by and silently watched Jonah, making him feel nervous. After the tank had been filled, Ray pointed to the dirty windscreen. 'Give that a clean for us. The back window as well.'

Jonah did as he was told, watching the two young men closely all the while. 'This car's fucking filthy,' Ray said to Kelvin, lightly kicking a side panel. 'Hey, Jonah, give the car a good wash as well.'

'I'm sorry, but we don't have that service here,' Jonah said.

'You don't have what? Can you try speaking proper?' Ray said, smiling at Kelvin.

Jonah was no fool. He knew that Ray was working up to trouble and didn't want to provoke him. 'We don't clean any cars here. Just the windscreen,' he explained. He held an open hand out. 'You need to pay me now. That's almost a full tank of petrol.'

'But I asked you to clean the car,' Ray said. 'I can't pay you for the petrol until you've cleaned the car. That's right, isn't it, Kel?'

Kelvin leaned against the bonnet. 'That's right. Fuck, Jonah, you've been working here long enough to know that. A full tank of petrol here comes with a free carwash. You stupid or something?'

Jonah looked over Kelvin, who was grinning widely. Kelvin was as stupid-looking as any person Jonah had seen. 'That's not right. We clean no cars here. This is Bobby Chuck's business and we offer no free service.'

'You do today,' Ray said. He opened the car door. 'If you don't want to wash the car for us, that's fine. We'll take the free tank of gas instead.'

Ray moved to get in the car. Jonah grabbed hold of the open car door. 'You can't be doing this, stealing from Mr Chuck. He's a good man.'

Ray grabbed Jonah by the lapels of his boiler suit and dragged him away from the car. Kelvin wrestled Jonah from behind and pinned his arms. 'You listen to me,' Ray spat. 'Don't you be telling me what I can and can't do, you swamp boong.' He shook Jonah. 'If it wasn't for silly old Chuck playing the do-gooder for you, this town would have been rid of you and the rest of them mongrels out at the river.'

'Leave him be!'

Ray turned and saw Bobby Chuck holding a tyre lever in one hand. 'Leave Jonah alone,' he repeated.

Kelvin released his grip on Jonah but Ray refused to do likewise. 'Fuck off, old man,' he said. 'I'll do what I like.'

'He says he won't pay,' Jonah said. 'The petrol money.'

'Oh, he'll fucking pay, alright,' Bobby said. He took a step closer to Ray. 'You let go of him now and pay the money I'm owed.'

Jonah was a little shocked. He'd never heard Bobby swear in all the years he'd worked for him.

'What if I don't want to pay?' Ray smirked.

Bobby raised the tyre lever above his head. 'If you don't pay me, I'll bring this down on you and crush your skull with it.'

Ray looked at Kelvin for support, who was nervously grinding his teeth. Bobby Chuck sensed the uncertainty in both young men and took advantage of their anxiety. 'Let Jonah go now and pay me and piss off. Or you'll have trouble.'

If the old man was bluffing, Ray thought, he was doing a good job of it. He released his grip on Jonah, pulled his wallet from his pocket, took out a bank note, screwed it into a ball and threw it at Bobby. 'There you are. The money for the petrol with some change. Use it to buy yourself a sheriff's badge.'

He got back into the car and roared away.

The two men worked quietly for the next hour or so before it was time for Bobby to leave for the day. He washed his oil-stained hands in the washroom and stripped himself of his boiler-suit. Underneath, he wore his second uniform of faded jeans and checked flannel shirt. He said goodbye to Jonah. He was about to leave and changed his mind.

'I'm really sorry for what happened today. That young Ray. He's a crazy one. The whole family are. But don't be worrying yourself over him, Jonah. He won't be back here. Not tonight. Ray runs a card game in the old shearing shed on the family property of a Friday night. He'll be kept busy with that. And I'm sorry for the language I used earlier. That's not me. None of it is. I just needed to put on some front, a bit of bluff. Just enough to be sure they doubted their own menace.'

Jonah waited until Bobby had turned away before he spoke. 'You shouldn't have done that, Bobby,' he said.

'Done what?' Bobby asked.

'What you did before. With the tyre lever. Standing up to them.'

Bobby was puzzled. 'Why not, Jonah? He was going to lay into you. The two of them, maybe. They would have given you a hiding.'

'Oh,' Jonah said, actually smiling. 'You're right there. Two young whitefellas, getting a bit of sport out of me. Yep, they would have enjoyed that, for sure.'

'Well,' Bobby asked. 'Why tell me to stay out of it? Would you rather me stand by and let them beat you?'

'That's right.'

'But why?' Bobby asked, frustrated.

Jonah created a fist and lightly punched his own chest as he spoke and raising his voice slightly. 'Because, Bobby, because,' he said rhythmically, 'because I am not some silly old boong. Today is my birthday and I am a man. And I have been a man for a long, long time. You're a good fella, Bobby, but this is not for you. It's for me to deal with this. Stand up for myself to them boys.'

For the remainder of the afternoon Jonah tinkered around the garage and served the occasional customer. He knew each of them by name and they knew Jonah, although few spoke to him other than to exchange small talk. Jonah didn't mind, seeing as he preferred his own company. He was about to close the garage when a driver pulled in for petrol. Jonah looked through the cracked windscreen while filling the tank. The driver was Marlene Conlon. Her father had been the minister at the church Jonah attended as a boy, along with other members of the river mob. Marlene was a couple of years older than Jonah and he'd never spoke to her at church. The Minister, her father, was a severe man who berated his parishioners each Sunday about the power of sin and the congregation's weakness in fighting it.

Walking home to the river camp one afternoon, Jonah had heard what he thought were the cries of an animal and followed them, along a narrow track into the bush. Had Jonah known what he was about to witness he'd have turned away, realising the danger of such a situation. But he was too late. In an opening between a stand of trees he looked into the eyes of Marlene Colon, on her back, almost naked, laying alongside a lay preacher from the church. She stared at Jonah until he turned and ran. He refused to return to church and rarely saw Marlene again. When he did come across her occasionally around town, Marlen didn't bother to look away or attempt to avoid Jonah. She didn't need to. She looked through him, for as far as she was concerned, Jonah barely existed.

He returned the petrol nozzle to the bowser and walked to the side of the car. Marlene wound down the window. She looked directly at Jonah just as she'd done thirty years earlier. It was a moment of shared knowing that disgusted her and made Jonah feel uneasy. She handed Jonah the cash for the petrol. By the time he'd returned with her change, the car was gone. He locked the garage, forgot his birthday gift, went back inside and retrieved the hunting knife and leather pouch. He didn't see Ray and Kelvin until it was too late for him to lock the front door on them.

'Hey,' Ray said, drawling. He was obviously drunk. 'That old prick, Bobby, has you on overtime. You know, I don't like him. The way he was threatening me today with that iron bar. I should have kicked his arse. You think so, Jonah?'

Jonah ignored the comment. 'What do you want here? I'm finished for the day.'

'We just come for some cigarettes,' Kelvin said. 'You have any?'

Jonah placed a packet of *Viscount* on the counter. 'There you are. You fellas need to leave. I have to be locking up now.'

'We'll have two packets,' Kelvin yelled.

'No, we won't,' Ray said. 'Jonah, we'll take a carton. Thank you, brother.'

Jonah was certain Ray wouldn't pay for the cigarettes. Being drunk also meant that he was more dangerous than usual. He'd have to give them the carton of cigarettes if he was to get rid of them. The cost would have to come out of his wages. He reached behind the counter, searching for a carton of cigarettes. The hunting knife spilled out of his jacket, onto the floor, and landed at Ray's feet.

'Hey, look at this baby,' Ray laughed. He took the knife out of the leather pouch. 'Oh, this is fucking beautiful. Kel, grab the cigarettes.'

'That is my knife,' Jonah said. 'You need to give it back to me.'

'Who says it's yours?' Ray said. 'I can't see your name on it.'

'It is mine,' Jonah insisted. 'Bobby gave that to me for my birthday. You need to give it back to me. Now.'

Jonah reached for the knife and Ray thrust it toward him. The point of the blade stopped a breath from Jonah's throat. He froze. 'You want it, Jonah. You'll have to take it off me,' Ray said.

Kelvin raised his hands in the air. 'Hey, take it easy, Ray. Jonah here is just a harmless Abo. Leave him be. You're cool, aren't you, Jonah? There's no trouble here.'

Jonah stepped away from the blade. 'This is my knife. For my birthday.'

'Give it back to him, Ray,' Kelvin said. 'It's poor Jonah's big day.'

'Get fucked, Kel. The knife is mine.' He winked at Jonah. 'I tell you what.' He took money from his wallet. 'Shout yourself a flagon of wine for your birthday. On me. Grab the smokes, Kel.'

An hour later Ray Jeans was holding court in the old shearing shed over a solid drink and a card game, for money. He held the hunting knife in his hand and showed the others how he had put it to Jonah's throat. 'You should have seen the look on the blackfella's face,' Ray said. 'He shit himself.'

The men were too busy rousing and drinking and slapping Ray on the back to hear the footsteps circling the wooden platform surrounding the shed. Eventually Kel suspiciously sniffed the cold night air.

'What's that smell?' he said.

Robin Cowcher

'There's no fucking smell except you,' Ray said. 'You should have had a tub before you come out here.'

'Speak for yourself, Ray. You're on the nose yourself.'

One of the other drinkers, Moe Grimes, who'd been the one asleep in the back of Ray's car earlier in the day, also smelled something in the air. 'It's petrol,' he said.

'Petrol?' Ray stumbled to the shed door and opened it. Jonah stood in the doorway with a lit kerosene lamp in one hand and a jerry-can in the other. Between Jonah and Ray the wooden boards were soaked in petrol. 'What the fuck?' Ray said.

'My hunting knife,' Jonah said. 'I've come for my knife.'

'Well, you can't have it,' Ray said. 'Fuck off before I kick your arse. What's with the petrol, you mad cunt?'

Jonah waved the kero lamp in the direction of the soaking petrol. Kelvin called out to Ray. 'Give him the fucking knife, Ray. The fumes on their own could blow us.'

The men screamed and shouted and argued amongst themselves before Ray caved in. Quicker than would have been expected. Kelvin threw the knife and pouch to Jonah. 'Now fuck off.' But Jonah wasn't satisfied with the knife alone. 'Your clothes. Take all your clothes off and throw them over here.'

The men swore and cursed some more at Jonah but were persuaded to do as he instructed once he moved the lamp closer to the spilt petrol. He gathered the clothes and boots and created a pyre on the gravel driveway. He tipped the last splash of the petrol onto the clothes and set them alight with a match.

'Hey,' a naked and freezing Ray called out to him. 'Don't you know that we'll be coming after you for doing this?'

Jonah swung the lamp from side to side. The flame danced. 'Oh, I know that. I know that real well, Ray. But I have my knife. And I'm a man.'

THE COOK

by David Whish-Wilson

A father is God to his son.

My father said that before I killed him, but he wasn't talking about us.

His own father. His father's father. His father's father's father, perhaps.

Said it before I pulled the trigger on his .303.

Today I leave Casuarina Prison after five years—no step-down into minimum.

But not because of what I've done — what I know.

My history as a speed cook, forced to stay in the SHU, with the psychos, peds and catamites, to keep me away from my suitors. There are five bikie mobs in Perth and they all want to own me, despite my history with the needle. I've avoided them because that part of my life, it's over. They aren't the kind to take no for an answer, but I'm not complaining. I haven't done the time hard, not like my earlier stretches. Not when even the screws have watched all four seasons of *Breaking Bad* — the same screws who call me Heisenberg with a mocking respect, although I was always more Jesse Pinkman than Walter White.

Their respect isn't for me, the waster, but for the science of the thing. The working with explosive materials in confined spaces. The alchemy, what I see as chemistry, following a recipe. The mystical transubstantiation of base materials into the manna of heaven, as another old crim described it.

I make no such claims myself. Starting with sulphate back in the eighties; bog-standard crank, learnt from a smuggled copy of Uncle Fester's Cookbook, whose recipes I have adapted, improved over the years, the ice I made was sought after by the criminal and social elite who could afford it.

I didn't come cheap, but that is simply the price of blood. I hear stories now and then. Like a gun manufacturer will hear stories. Like the brother of a cell-mate of mine who after a three-day binge injected his cock and lost both legs to gangrene. Stories of psychosis and ruin. Violence and poverty visited upon innocents. You get the picture, and why I've had enough.

The only man I confided my decision to is the prison psych. Nothing to do with going straight, or walking the line. I told him that the very worst things I have done were done with the best of intentions.

Isn't that punishment enough?

My second son, Danny. The only person in the world I want to see. Waiting for me outside the prison gates, sun shearing off the bonnet of his Valiant Charger.

This is a good sign. On the prison wireless I've heard Danny's running wild, working as a deckie for Gary Warner, although everyone knows what that means. Warner is the only non-bikie crim who, because of his Calabrian connections, gets to make speed and ice and ecstasy, distributed through the insulated Italian smack networks.

Warner is the same bloke who most pundits think offed my first son, Kevin, those five years back, after he ripped him off for a kilo of pure.

That Danny still has the Valiant means something. It was my gift, once he got his licence, to celebrate his coming out of foster care, and it means that he hasn't gone too far off the rails.

Danny was thirteen the last time I went inside. *Keep your friends close, and enemies closer*. The kind of Machiavellian dictum that a thirteen year old needs to understand. Last thing I said to him. Danny never visited me in jail because I wouldn't allow it.

If he had, I wouldn't have told him any different. Play it smart, but don't let them stand over you. Once you're down, life will keep kicking.

Danny doesn't get out of the car. He's seen detective inspector Brett Ogilvie, smoking a rollie beside his fleet vehicle Falcon, perk of his shift to Federal Police. He's parked, deliberately, behind a black TRG mini-tank, stationed there in case of a riot. Like the US President's wartime speeches, back-dropped by rows and rows of jug-jawed soldiers, a wallpaper of quiet menace.

This whole prison release thing is a movie cliché, but there you have it. The hard-looking kid in a muscle-car, the concerned cop, the sunlight on my pale skin, my squinting eyes.

Danny passes me some Oakley sunglasses, and the world goes feather-soft. Both of us ignore Ogilvie as we cruise down to the main road, but as we turn left towards Fremantle a black Hummer limo enters from the right. I keep my head down but can't avoid Mastic's mutt face framed by panels of tinted glass, in the rear. He simply points at me, as the sergeant-at-arms of The Nongs is given to do, master to his minions. Mastic will have chilled beer in there, the kind that tastes like chemical soup, and some hard-faced prossies with plastic tits.

'Should we go back?' Danny asks. 'I been hearin…' 'That he's been protecting me. I know. It's bullshit.' 'I forgot to ask. You want to drive?'

'No. You drive.'

I saw it in Danny the moment he picked me up, but I hoped I was wrong. Two minutes inside his flat proved me right. Fit-pack on the coffee table, base of an upturned Coke can for a spoon. He worked the powder into the water and drew up a shot, passed it to me. I shook my head, looked at him coldly. Baby blue eyes and ice-cream skin, hair like finely blown toffee. Like his mother.

He looks hurt. All his childish needing to please, there on the surface. Softness, vulnerability, and it catches in my gut.

Because where I've come from, the first instinct is to squash it, in yourself and others. What the psychs call learned behaviour.

And then it comes through, the deeper and stronger, longest held. The moment of his birth.

My quiet, tender child. My second son.

Working the fit into the serpentine vein on the back of his hand, the puff of blood in the glass, driven home.

He smiles and caps the fit, lights a Styvie, slumps in his chair.

I can't take my eyes off him. My youngest boy, grown into a man. I barely notice what my hands are doing, although he watches closely. He is both in the first flush, but long gone, and yet there is time to catch him. After all these years, it's not far to go. To follow my child. That he not be alone. Wherever he assumes he's going.

Thinking that he knows where I've been.

It's only when his friends arrive that the trouble starts. Two rat-faced morons that are clearly his best mates, kids Kevin's age, early twenties.

Juvie boys, the kind that Warner attracts. Strangely androgynous and PVC white, all the usual tatts and prominent labels. Dickhead hip-hop on the iPod dock. Porn on the laptop. Ice in the pipe. Laughter with a dull edge of malice. Eyes vague and fierce. They repulse me, disappoint me, but not only because I fear their unpredictability. The kind I've been among these past five years. The kind as likely to stick a pencil in a sleeping man's ear, heel of the hand forcing it home, as to suck him off for a cigarette.

They can see what Danny is. Not like Kevin.

'Danny, you ready?'

Danny takes the pipe and sucks it down. The smack was strong, and not because I'm green again. I can hardly lift my head. Danny is just as greedy on the pipe as they are, something I wouldn't have expected.

'Ready for what?'

'Never mind, old man. Stay here an' nod off.'

Danny can't meet my eyes. Starts gathering his shit: ciggies, wallet, knife. The other one is back from the bedroom, lugging a green sports bag heavy with iron.

I shake my head, start to rouse myself.

I have left Danny with his brother's world, a world that Kevin belonged to, mine before him. I feel like stabbing my fit into the kid's eyes. He can sense it, too, and laughs.

'Yo, Danny, your dad is *fierce*.'

Where I want to go. The only place I've been where my radar doesn't ping, once, twice every minute. Where I can sleep easy. The place where my father lies unburied, at the bottom of a mineshaft. not a place I ever expected to yearn for.

But there is peace there.

I wait behind the wheel of the stolen Camry sedan while they do the armed robs — three of them. Two servos and a late night chemist. Not a few k's from where they live.

Such is the life of a moron.

They whoop and rap and smoke the short drive back to the port city, down along the eerily quiet Capo D'Orlando Drive, through gritty sulphur halos and clanking marinas and the smell of diesel and antifoul and rotting seaweed. We park before the long line of Warner's crayboats and trawlers, strung with red and green halogen caps, decks awash in hard fluorescent light.

Danny and his friends divvy up the eight hundred cash and transfer the weapons from the stolen car to a nearby Falcon ute, the rush of the thieving gone now they're at work.

Prison full of kids like this. There because they want to be, the stupid ones to prove themselves to others, the smarter for themselves.

But Danny's not prison material, and his friends aren't the kind to stand by him, should he be marked out for special attention.

I hadn't allowed Danny to talk about what he was doing for Warner, either in the car or at his flat. Ogilvie would certainly have bugged the car, perhaps the flat. But I let the others in the Camry bray how they worked the presses for Warner, who'd been importing high-end E from Amsterdam, cutting it down by 50% and re-pressing his own pills with his own logo: Jagger lips.

The kids worked the presses all night, another shift worked days, cray season nearly over. Warner's fleet could easily get out into international water, to trawl up submersible barrels tagged with homing devices, his MO now for close to two decades.

Danny and the kids expect me to take the Camry and leave, but when I don't, there is anticipation in their eyes. Mastic has offered to knock Warner for me, but because I've always refused, it's assumed that I intend to do him myself.

Warner has never denied killing my son, Kevin.

Warner strides down the dock towards me, white gumboots stained with fish-guts and scale, black boardies and skin-tight bluey, bunched forearms and hairy hunched shoulders, the body of a worker.

Danny stays beside, but the other kids draw back.

Warner right in my face, stale sweat and ashtray mouth, flecks of fish blood on his cheek, eyes yellow beneath the sulphur light, moths batting around our heads.

Ogilvie will be watching from nearby.

He knows our history, was a beat copper when Warner and I ran plantations for Joe Italiano in the Gascoyne. Warner married into the family, took on the fishing licences as both a cover and a going concern, has done well, never gone to jail.

I've gone the way of most. Habit. Jail. Habit. Jail.

But along the way I've taken on the trade, become the best at what I do.

A good cook is excused things that put others in shallow graves.

Except for one thing.

Warner puts out his hand, but he's so close it's more like a jab to the stomach.

Ogilvie will be watching, long-lens camera at his eyeball.

But Ogilvie is not the only one watching. Danny flinches when I take Warner's hand, something that is noticed by Warner. 'You got work to do?'

Danny's face is unreadable, until he meets my eye. Disappointment. Disbelief. A flash of something else.

I have chosen Warner.

Had in fact chosen him years earlier, made a promise of sorts, when an emissary of Warner's was transferred into the SHU. A wiry old Noongar crim, with blurred tattoos and oiled rockabilly hair, large fighter's hands. He told me about Danny, his message not couched in threat. Said Warner thought I'd like to know. Because of that unspoken history of ours. Fathers both dockworkers, did time together at Freo jail, drifted into the only union that would have them, the Painters & Dockers, before my dad went bush. Did he want me to hire Danny, or fuck him off?

Warner could see that Danny was no hard nut, had his father's weakness for the powder, but missed his father's luck. I say luck, because like most junkies my age, it's always the people around me who die, people like Danny's mother, so many others. I survive, like a curse.

But not Danny. He was headed one of two ways — neither good.

Hire him, I'd said. Then nothing else. No news. No threats, or further importuning.

I'd appreciated that. And I had my own reasons for wanting to be close to Warner.

I go back to Danny's flat and have a shot, drift quietly in my body, seated slumber, nodding bringing me round. Hours pass like the years have passed, my whole fucking life, sleepless but asleep, the old anaesthetic.

The deal is good. Warner's set-up is good. I'll be making MDMA at nights on a customised trawler, out on the Sound, when it's still. Plenty of ventilation, all the newest kit. The precursors there, dropped off in the shipping lanes, direct from India.

Ogilvie can't get to Warner, not with his connections. Warner has men in the Ports Authority, the local drug squad. The Federal coppers would work alone for this reason, but they would need boats and choppers to get to the floating lab, and Warner would hear.

Warner is also safe from The Nongs and the others, because of his father-in-law, even if I'm not. Mastic has boasted widely that if I don't work for him, then I won't work for anybody. Has put it about that I owe him, for his protection inside, and now he'll have to demonstrate that he isn't full of shit. His signature demonstration involves a ballpein hammer.

I'll live on another boat, nearby the lab, safe as long as I don't leave the port. I've told Warner that I'll work for a year, pocket the money, take Danny and head elsewhere, up North, or New Zealand, start again.

He doesn't trust me, but that's no surprise. It's still worth his while.

I'll be close to him, and I'm a patient man.

The explosion at the port rocks the apartment, sets clarions in the street to wailing. From the kitchen I see flames down on Capo D'Orlando, fizzing white, incendiary secondary detonations, oil black streaks over the watercolour night sky.

The moment I think of Danny my legs weaken, and then I see him limp into the street. Vomit into a gutter. Limp towards the Charger, pop the boot, drop in a canvas bag, lean his weight on the closed trunk.

I understand. Feel a surge of panic. Start grabbing stuff, hearing Danny's key in the lock.

Turn, stand to face him. 'Warner's dead. Danny? *Warner.*'

His face tells the truth. He's burned on his neck, suppurating red blisters, what looks like a broken wrist wedged into his armpit, pupils dilated, in shock.

Eyes already on the coffee table, the fit-pack and powder.

I sit him down and fix him, watch his pupils screw inward, take the Charger keys from his hand and help him to his feet.

Dawn finds us out in the mallee scrub, beyond the wheat-belt and into cattle country, headed north. The dirt reddens and the heat falls hard and granite mesas rise out of the plains and dry gullies. Beneath the gnarled trunks of the mallee and currajong and corkwood the horizon fills with a floating carpet of pink and white everlastings, surreal.

Danny is in a bad way, and I fix him twice in cutaways beneath the feathery shade of beefwood and quandong, but then the packet is done. I'd stopped at a 24 hour chemist on the way out of Bassendean, had bought downers, painkillers, burn-salves, bandages, whatever they had. The blankets from the beds in the flat. Stuff from the cache of stolen property in the bedroom cupboards, to trade perhaps, some cameras, binoculars and a telescope, a fucking leaf-blower, some mobiles and laptops, miscellaneous tools.

That was before I looked inside the bag in the boot. Saw the cash, banded and loose, range of colours, no time to count it — and a handgun, a .38 S&W snubnose, no bullets.

I pay for petrol with cash at Payne's Find roadhouse, buy food for a few days, put us back on the highway north. The vintage two-door Charger is a distinctive ride, but eats the road between the towns, a few more hours we're in Cue. I take a dirt road before we hit the main street, buildings like a stage-set in a Hollywood mirage, then head west towards the Rock, parachute of dust curling over the floodplain of poverty bush and salt-grass, the abandoned gold diggings of Big Bell on the horizon north.

We get to Walga Rock when the sun is overhead, Danny still dazed and mute, angry because I'd chosen Warner, but afraid of what he'd done. The Rock slopes high and red beside the road, granite dome filling the sky, plated like a half-buried turtle, a lone wedge-tail circling in the higher thermals. I drive the opposite direction over the graded lip of red gravel and twenty yards into the bush. From here on there are no roads. I return to the lip and build it up again, sweep over our tracks with a mistletoe switch. It's slow going, lost in the low scrub, every now and then getting out to climb a beefwood, trying to catch a glimpse of the blue-grey monolith to the east, no name beyond what my father and his father called it, home.

It takes four hours to drive the twenty k, at walking speed. Danny is too sick to get out and guide, and not wanting to stake a tyre, I circle round the fallen acacia and dry gullies over plains of purple mulla mulla and flannel bush and everlastings, knee-deep dry grass, plovers and bush-quail sailing off in brief clucking parabolas, waves of locusts rising like a parting sea. It's hot on the vinyl seats, but the setting sun to the west is the best compass I have. Working slowly through a clump of fruiting quandong, hundreds of green and red budgerigar chirruping above us, I see the sparrowhawk and know we're close. It glides above us, taking a good close look through unblinking eyes, circling before rising off the scrubline in an effortless arc. I remember that the sparrowhawk feeds on the swallows at the rock, and follow it. Soon the broad red flank of the granite monolith looms before us, a couple of hundred metres high, unlikely as always in the broad flat plain, the red dirt around it as trackless as I'd hoped. We circle round to the eastern side, into the shade, looking for my father's camp, marked by a screen of casuarina and the quandong planted by my grandfather, its seeds buried beside jam wattle saplings, to feed off its roots.

I drive the Charger into the cleft of rock that curls beneath an overhang, invisible from the air, and turn off the ignition. Immediately the eerie silence settles over us, just the ticking of the overworked engine.

I help Danny climb out of his seat and sit him against the smooth trunk of a leaning redgum. Light him a cigarette and set off to get firewood, dragging the dry mallee boughs caked in dirt, a few sticks of sandalwood. I set a fire in the cave, in the ancient fireplace used for so many thousands of years that the rock has melted into a scoop, ochre handprint of a Wadjari child on the smooth wall above. When I leave the cave Danny's still slumped against the tree, but has lifted his sunnies, watching a young male bower-bird perform for him, flacking its wings in a fan dance, hopping on its thin legs.

The anger that made Danny do to Warner what I wouldn't is gone now. Won't meet my eye.

'What's that?' he asks.

'Bowerbird. Young male. No pink on its back. He's trying out his moves on you.'

'So I shouldn't laugh.'

'How's your neck? Your arm?' 'Flies are bad.'

'Wipe your arse with your shirttails, keeps the flies away from your face.'

'Really?'

'No.'

I lift the collar of his shirt and pull back the gauze on his burn, still angry red but the blisters have stopped weeping. Important to keep the flies off, so I set about applying the salve over the dry powder I'd caked it with earlier; lay down some new gauze.

'That one of your dad's sayings?' he asks. 'Good guess.'

'Don't piss on my back and tell me it's raining.' 'You remember that?'

'Sure. He's tighter than a stocking on a chicken's lip. Face like a pox-doctor's clerk.'

Image of my father, face red with drink, propped up at the Fremantle Workers Club, the idiom of his generation bustling in the air, laughter.

Before he went mad, wouldn't leave his room, pissed off out here with his rifle and a single bag of clothes.

'I ever tell you about this place?' 'No.'

'You need water?' 'I need hammer.' 'None left.'

Danny's face goes ugly for a moment, brought back to normal with a strained effort. 'S'alright. My fault. All this.'

'Wait here. Watch the show.'

The bower bird, who's been silent and watching while we talk, resumes his dance as I leave the camp, zebra finches techno-thrumming in the mistletoe by the cave. I walk up onto the rock, and climb through the fading light onto a ledge that looks over the desert, mallee scrub to the horizon in every direction, a mob of kangaroo grazing near the soak. The gnamma holes on the rock still hold fetid water, tadpoles squirming in the shallows; poor man's caviar, my dad used to call them, swallowed them live and whole, as his father had taught him. Beneath a slab of red granite streaked with long quartz veins I pull out the oilcloth and sports bag, shovel and pick, ammo box filled with Dad's cutlery, ledgers, tools.

It takes two trips but I get the lot down to camp, leave it near the old fireplace, coals glowing. Unwrap the .303 from its oilcloth. Grease is clean and golden. No sign of rust. Not enough moisture in the dry desert air. Bullets dull brass in their cardboard cartridges, couple dozen of them. I load one into the breech and sight on the mob of goats that have come down the rock to observe, the billy goat coughing, staring at me down the sight, never seen a human before. I sight on the smallest kid, take in his colours, for later, when the food runs out. My father lived out here on goat and grass seed johnny- cakes for months at a time. Quandong in season. Tadpoles. Frogs. Bush turkey. His father before him. Famous among local prospectors. Had been so confident he'd found El Dorado he'd traded a ten ounce nugget for a crate of sherry, before the hole went dry. It was when Grandpa died that my father followed him out here, worked the hole deeper into the granite and greenstone bands, gelignite and pick and shovel, mercury and cyanide extracted, right through summer. Dug out enough to pay for his smokes and bullets, but not much else. Everything listed in a shivery hand in his ledgers.

I take the rifle and the shovel and go and dig out the soak, hefting the dry sand that becomes damper, the rifle laid over a rock beside me.

The soak begins to fill with muddy water, and I keep digging. I had a lot of time to think on the drive up. We could live out here, make furtive trips into town, pay with cash. This is somebody's land, part of a cattle station the size of Victoria, no reason the owners would ever find us. My father and his father had never cared whose land it was, had always kept the .303 handy. This wasn't the kind of country you walked up on someone unannounced, even if you were the owner. Hunters out here. Prospectors. Fugitives.

But Warner is still alive, and Warner knows my father's diggings were near Cue. The logical place for a city-boy to run, with Danny.

Warner knew that I was going to have a crack at him. Most likely, he would have offed me after a couple of good batches. But he wouldn't have expected it from Danny.

Cue was eighty k to the east. Lot of country between us. We would probably be safe here.

Not a lot of other options.

It's a feudal world, the drug trade. My only other choice is to go to Mastic, bow and scrape, swear undying loyalty. Hope he can protect us.

Or go dog for Ogilvie, and hope for the same.

But no legs in either option. Once I'm no use, they'll burn me to trade up, part of the game.

The sun has nearly gone and the light softens in the warm shade. Tiny tree frogs begin their migration from the gnamma holes to the grass and nearest scrub. A babbler singing on the rock. The sparrowhawk flies over for another look.

I watch the water drain into the soak clear and sweet, lob the shovel into the grass and carry the rifle over to the camp. Danny's still leaning against the gum, staring up at the rock, at the fat retreating tail of a giant bungarra, belly scraping rhythmically on the rock, flicking tongue tasting the air.

'It walked right past me. Wasn't scared at all.'

'Top of the food chain. Probably the same lizard I used to see here, twenty years ago. Dad used to shoot goat for it. The odd feral cat. Lives in a cleft of rock up there. A good sign. Keeps the snakes away.'

'Talkin like a bushie already. What's the plan? Stay here for the night? I'm gettin real sick.'

'Don't be an arse. If you'd killed Warner, we might go back, one day. Years from now.'

'A hospital. Morphine, for my bust wrist.'

'Not a chance. We're here until I figure it out. I've got some pills.' Danny's face turns ugly again, and I know the look.

'Can you walk?'

'Sure. But I need some pills.'

'One pill, every few hours.'

Danny's first time coming off. I've done it a hundred times, maybe more, and it will be hard to watch him suffer.

He thinks it's bad already.

Before it starts I want to show him the mine. We walk through fifty yards of scrub, ancient trees evenly spaced, has the feel of an orchard planted by a careful hand, everything radiant in the last warm light, to the edge of the mineshaft.

'Careful.'

My hand across Danny's chest. Just a big hole in the ground, vertical, my grandfather's hand-sawed boughs framing the edges, perfectly square, dug out with a pick and shovel.

'Why here?'

I shake my head. 'I've always wondered that. Don't think my dad knew either. Just that it produced a bit, for his dad. Between them, they worked it for close to twenty years.'

'He died out here, didn't he?'

I ignore the question, looking down into the hole. 'We'll have a better look tomorrow. But first, what my father told me when I was your age. Don't wander. At first, all the trees look the same. It's easy to get lost, and hard to get found. In this heat, you'll last two days without water…three at the most.'

'But the rock.'

'You can be fifty metres from the rock in this scrub, not see it. Just do as I say. Don't wander off.'

'Ok.'

We're nearly back to the rock when I hear the chopper. It's gone dark enough for the searchlights to stand out against the red horizon, the clear twin beams of white light sweeping towards us.

We make it to the cave before the police chopper sights us, turning slowly around the edge of the rock, looking for our camp, but the searchlights make one thing clear.

Either Warner has a mate in the local coppers, out doing his bidding, perhaps even up there with a rifle, or else the fire at the wharf got too big for Warner to control. Meaning there's a general manhunt out for us. Meaning every copper in the state is on our tail.

If it's Warner pulling the strings, and they find us, we're dead.

Warner's name is on the line, and he will never give up. Plenty that went up in smoke, not covered by insurance.

Beyond forgiveness now, or recompense. Even for a prized cook.

I dose Danny with three pills at once, bed him down in a nest of blankets, leave him a pot of water, the rest of the food, scratch crude directions into the cave floor, should I never return.

Walk out into the night, rifle over my shoulder, the full moon rising over the eastern horizon, enough light to drive by.

It takes me five hours to make the road, following our earlier tracks, another hour to get into the Cue town site, make the roadhouse just before it closes. Fill up the Charger, pay using Danny's credit card, make sure my picture on the servo surveillance video is clear. Do the same at the bottle shop. Hope to Christ the coppers don't get me in town. I'll have to go down shooting. The strong possibility that one of them is owned by Warner. Don't want to be beaten to death in the Cue cells. Don't want to give up Danny's location. Don't want to not give it up, under torture — leave him out there alone, helpless.

I make small-talk with the bottle-shop owner, mention I'm camping at Walga Rock, take my half-carton and leave. Watch from my car to see if he runs to the phone.

He doesn't, which is not a good sign. Coppers are looking, but not asking.

I return along the dusty track beneath the risen moon and make camp not far from Walga Rock. A big fire, within plain sight of the road, near the car. Pile a few bags under the last two blankets, on the ground by the fire, two sleeping scarecrows, then walk back to the road with the leaf-blower, use it to blow away the car-tracks into the first fifty metres of bush the other side. When I've built up the graded lip again and I'm sure that our track is covered, I retreat back to the nearest flank of Walga Rock with the rifle, spend a night shivering and watching the road, herd of goats using the wallaby path behind me, coughing and snorting, my smell like an odd dream among them. I leave the rock only to keep the fire at the camp going, the urge to lie down and sleep strong.

Back in my stone eyrie I keep myself occupied cleaning the .303 by moonlight, with screwdriver and strips of my shirt, hope to hell the sight is still good. Count the stars coming out as the moon sinks to the horizon, as the inky darkness settles for an hour before the first flushes of dawn, there behind the distant lights of Cue.

I hear the chopper just before the sun spills red over the horizon, high up in the dark sky, just the distant syncopation among the winking stars, one of them moving slowly around the rock. I crawl beneath the nearest wedge of granite, to mask me from their infra-red, and settle down to wait. I'd placed the two swags as near the fire as possible, the whole camp glowing white on their screen.

It's working as I hoped. One of Warner's copper stooges in Perth, alerting him to the time and place of Danny's credit card use, last night. The chopper sent out to confirm the campsite. Warner likely on a light plane these past hours, Perth to Meekatharra, the short drive from there to Cue.

He'll be coming armed, in company. He'll want his money back, but this isn't about money.

An execution. An example. Done himself.

The chopper circles for a while then heads back to the town, dropping in altitude. I hunker down on the cold granite ledge and draw a bead over the plain, looking for plumes of dust.

The thought of Danny, probably awake now, shivering and sick. The certain knowledge that if I die, he dies too.

The last of us. The only good one.

I'm trying, but it doesn't feel real. The .303 heavy in my hands, the rifle my father taught me to use, when I was Danny's age.

And always the question I've been asking myself, ever since I decided to follow Danny — to never leave him, until he's safe from my world, from me, my good intentions.

At what point did I pass from being The Son, to The Father? It wasn't at the boys' birth, or even during their childhood. I was no real parent. Kevin always a pain in the arse. But Danny, never far from my mind. Knowing that until I find a place for him somewhere safe, I will not be able to die in peace.

Because my father did not die in peace.

The moment of his death the answer to my question. The moment I pulled the trigger, his eyes on mine, but grateful, I passed from being the son to the father. A father in a fatherless world. The godless world that he had lived in, when his father had died. What my father meant.

My father had been out here, dying, alone, when I found him.

The cancer, right through him by the time I arrived, just out on remand, come to collect something I'd left, the only bloke I could trust. He hadn't told anyone he was dying. He didn't have any meds. No transport to get into town. Too weak to walk the twenty k to the track, to hitch a ride.

It was already too late. The depth of his suffering. The sounds he made, like a flayed animal. The cancer in his brain. Helpless in his agony. I broke parole and stayed with him. Couldn't leave him to go to town, for help, too far gone. Made him broth that he couldn't swallow.

Fed him my own pills, useless.

Then the moment came. He was ready. Eyes became clear for a moment, drawn out of his delirium by the pain. Lost. Confused. Understood where he was. What was happening. His last act of will. Told me to do it. His own hands, no good.

Told me that I could do it.

I knelt before him on the cave floor, the .303 barrel in his mouth, his eyes on mine, watering, afraid. A paste of snot and blood, mixed with the red dirt, in his hair, his eyes, his mouth, in his bedding, all over his skin.

He said it then. 'A father is God to his son.'

I hear the Hilux engine before I see it, the plume of red dust rising out of the riverbed, settling over the red gum and casuarina grove, the car parked there amid the cover. One vehicle. No chopper. Cops keeping it at arm's length. Warner and one other, a Maori bloke I know, Morgan, who knows me, a good bloke who's come to do me in. Both armed with shining new shotties, a Sunday stroll, walk in the park, hunting the junkie and his junkie son, their navy blue jumpsuits like coppers' or miners' uniforms, black boots and caps, should there be any witnesses.

No witnesses out here.

I wait until they're in a sparse patch of cynic grass framed by a field of white everlastings, no cover beyond a few crumbling termite nests, shoot Morgan first, the crosshairs on his chest true, swing the bead onto Warner, who's pitched into the dirt, put a bullet into his shoulders, load another, put two more into each of them, watch their skulls burst like puffballs, red spores settling over the dirt, then start running, down the flank of the covering rock, towards the dried riverbed, to get in behind their vehicle, in case there's a driver.

There isn't. The Hilux is parked on a carpet of casuarina needles, the tracks of emu and roo and goat in the dried mud around. Windows down, passenger seat reclined, Warner having snoozed on the drive in, the bastard.

Doesn't look like a rental. Or a copper's car, on loan. In the glovebox I find the rego—a company car, Styx Gold Ltd, from a nearby mine, an Italiano family company.

Iced coffee cartons on the floorpan, some bacon egg roll wrappers, breath mints, Warner's cigarettes.

On the back seat, an overnight bag, two new sleeping bags, dunny paper, some cash in a bum-bag, wank mags, a blue tarp and two shovels, a jerry-can of fuel.

Warner no mug.

He'd make me dig our grave, mine and Danny's, pile on wood then pour on the fuel. Burn us into ashes and bone rubble, cover us over.

Gone forever.

I park the Hilux fifty metres into the bush, walk back over our track, build up the graded lip of gravel road and use the leaf-blower to cover our trail. The Valiant is waiting hidden in the river bed; its rego plates in the tray of the Hilux.

Warner sits beside me on the drive to the rock, buckled in, reclined, the other bloke in the tray, wrapped in the tarp. Both of them bled out already, into the dirt.

I want to keep this car, for later. An Italiano company vehicle, unlikely they'll claim it as missing.

Would raise too many questions.

No sign of the chopper either. Same reason. The slightest sniff of something gone wrong, Warner's stooges will abandon him, start covering their tracks, deleting searches from computers, wiping the flight-logs of choppers, until his body is found.

But it will never be found.

Danny takes one look at what's inside the Toyota and says, 'Oh, what a feeling.'

Late afternoon. All day driving and walking. Parking the Hilux in the cave, before I walk back to Walga Rock to collect the Charger.

Now Warner and Morgan are in the front seat of the Valiant, strapped in, sightless eyes staring over the bonnet, beginning to smell bad. Danny stands aside and smokes, says nothing as I roll the Valiant, slowly, carefully, over the lip of the mineshaft, wanting it to slide,

which it does, crashing once or twice on the way down.

I have no idea how deep the shaft is, and I will never know. Danny helps me drag the lighter firewood and tip it in. I put whole dried boughs down, mallee, beefwood, sandalwood, whatever is at hand. Pour over the fuel, follow it with a burning torch of poverty bush, stand back as the whump of heat rises in a vertical column of shimmering clear.

Keep feeding the fire, the compressed explosion of the Charger's tank, the sound of crumbling rock, superheated, the support boughs burning through.

The work of generations, collapsing in on itself, spume of red dust rising out of the shaft.

An end to it.

I am tired and covered in blood, dirt, charcoal. Haven't slept for close to sixty hours. We retreat to the cave. No words are necessary. We'll camp here, a week or two, perhaps a month. I'll hunt and cook. Danny will get clean.

Then we'll move. Enough cash to last a year, if we're careful.

A new start. New Zealand. Different line of work. Set Danny up with some kind of trade. Sit back and give him a chance.

The light in the cave is soft and red, like a child's crayon drawing. There's nothing to do now but sleep, rest, live my father's hermit life for a while, walk the rock, feed the bungarra, watch the light over the desert change as the gnamma holes dry up, as the birds fly to the coast.

I feel it for the first time in a long while, my eyes upon my son, feeding the fire: my father's presence in the cave with us, and it's not the violence of our last moments which haunts me, but the feeling that he is looking over us, perhaps, and then I am asleep.

THE TWO-DAY ROOM

by Julia Prendergast

Clare sits very still and thinks carefully about what Jem said—the two-day room. She wonders if it's possible—two days, to kill off this hideous yearning. It's too intense. It's not sustainable. Already she understands it's too much. She knows with a clear conviction that she otherwise felt was slipping—if she's not sure the two-day room will solve things... she should end this right now.

She wonders what Jem has in mind. What does the two-day room look like? Can she have too much, for two days only, in the two-day room, and leave it there? Be done with this as if enough were enough. Return to her life unscathed.

It's too much, she said. I'm strong but I can't do this kind of too-muchness.

Two days, he said: We can lock ourselves away for two days, a two-day room, and see what becomes. We won't go there if you don't want to.

Go where? She thinks. Is this a script? Clare laughed, thinking about how this would go down in the tearoom at work. The nurses would love this. Tash would be, like: *Where does he get this shit? Two-day room—I mean, please...*

It's a gorgeous old pub—a spacious old room in a restored hotel, wood panelling and chandeliers, textured wallpaper, black languid swirls, carved timber wall-lamps. Clare pretends that this elsewhere-place is back in time, unrelated to her life with Cliff. Everything smells of sandalwood. She sinks against the giant feather pillows, stroking the mohair blankets, pale yellow, rubbing her bare feet against the thick, creamy sheets. There are doors to the balcony and the sea is right there, across the service road. Near the door, there is a chaise lounge with blue velvet upholstery, royal blue, brass studs. Lying there, Clare can see the sea and she never wants to go home.

Jem calls downstairs at regular intervals. The other man brings prawns and oysters, whole fish. He passes Jem drinks on a round, bronze tray—a never-ending booze-train, wine, gin and tonic, Cointreau shots, Bloody Marys, scotch for Jem. The man loiters in the doorway as if he's waiting to be invited in. He and Jem share a nod, smirking. They touch hands. It's not a handshake but something else altogether, fleeting and yet clutching. Sometimes, in the parched night, Clare hears shuffling feet near the doorway, the rattle of keys or coins in a pocket. Did Jem remember to lock the door? Clare wakes him in the briny-light of nearly-dawn. *Are you friends with that man?* She asks, palms flat against his chest. *He looked like he wanted to come in. Why did you take his hand so… tenderly? Have you had women here before? Is he part of it? Is he…*

Jem jerks himself upright, his fingers gouge her underarms, hooking deeper as he steers her across the room like a surfboard. At first, she thinks he's aroused—she's not prepared for the anger. He thwacks her face against the round mirror of the Tiger Oak dresser. Her mouth is open, slightly. Her front teeth and lips smack against the glass—the spherical mirror is like a face, domed. Her tooth aches. Is it chipped? She can taste blood. His face appears beside hers. *What do you see, Clare? What do you make of me, huh?*

Jem lets go abruptly, panting madly, dribbling into his beard. He walks across to the poster bed, also Tiger Oak. *It's quarter sawn*, says Jem, wiping his mouth, calmer now but still puffing, delivering his lines as if he's practiced them. He runs his hand down the post tenderly—as if he would never drag a woman by her underarms and slam her face against a mirror. Clare crosses her arms over her chest, clutching her small breasts, fingertips reaching under her armpits, crying, willing herself to stop, making a medium-pitch humming sound to quell a real outburst. Jem runs his hands up and down the bedpost. Clare looks enviously at the slick wood, his hands. She notes her quickening breath. Her desire sickens her. She makes a sound between humming and crying, her mouth watery as if she might vomit. She is deeply frightened. *I should*, she says. She stops, checking herself. *I'm cold*, she adds.

She reaches for the pale-yellow blanket, marvelling at the mohair as she wraps it around herself like a shawl, crying again and humming, only more softly now. She stares at the ceiling, so high, like cream-coloured sky. She longs, suddenly, for home, for her pubescent teenagers and their overflow of hormones. It seems so pure now. Crunchy sheets. Bring it on. Who cares? That's so normal. She's desperate for Cliff of the needy eyes—for clean longing. Her everyday life seems so safe, so buoyant—predictable demands, steady desire without the brutality. She wants to rest her head against Cliff's chest and listen to his fluttery, unfettered breathing. From here on, she'll be grateful that she knows how things will play out. She'll forget this, whatever *this* is. She looks at Jem briefly and then at the faraway ceiling.

Come here, says Jem in his black-eyed poet's voice. His hand remains planted against the bedpost. With his other hand, his thumb, he wipes the blood at her lip, lingering at the exposed flesh, swollen and throbbing. She flinches, turns her head away. He takes her hair at the nape of her neck, like a ponytail but yanking. He lets go of the bedpost, takes her breast in his hand, bends his head and takes her nipple in his mouth, too insistently. *It hurts*, she says, drawn back to crying, wondering how she'll get out of here, wondering if there is worse to come, wondering what worse would look like. She draws a quick breath, the air like a blade against her torn lip.

He straightens up, plants kisses along her collarbone. *The quarter-sawn method reveals the medullary rays in the wood, he says slowly. The distinct stripes add the individual character. It's like you can see inside the timber. As if it were living flesh.*

Medullary—she says. She wonders if it's even a word. *Is…* she begins to ask, but checks herself, taking another sharp breath, recalibrating, the air electric against her jagged tooth. She forces a stiff smile, flinches, licking the exposed lip. She casts her gaze downward—not her head—he has control of her neck, he puppeteers it with her hair. She can only control her sightline.

Could you live without your children? He says. *I want you to myself.* He kisses her battered lip, very softly. Two days is not enough.

In the relentless waking he has asked her this before, more than once. Could you vanish from that life? She had kissed him in lieu of answering, the first time, taken his penis in her mouth, the second. Today he has her hair. Today he split her lip.

I can't think of you with another man's children. I can't deal, he says, muddy eyes catching glint—a thin band of concentrated gold across the width of his eyeball—like cat's eye, band of fire.

Crying steadily, biting the fleshy inside of her mouth with her rough tooth, she lifts her head to kiss him. He bends his head rather than loosening his hold on her hair. Despite the perturbing amber of his too-serious eyes, she holds his gaze, too frightened to look away.

By day five, Jem can't resist the water. The wind has switched. The surf is writhing and his eyes are elsewhere, momentarily. Clare pretends to be sleeping. After he leaves, she gathers her things hurriedly and rushes to the door. It's locked. He's locked her in. She didn't hear the locking. Is it self-locking?

She goes to the balcony, turns right, tries the door of the next room—locked, heavy curtains closed and cobwebbed. The room at the far end is also locked, padlocked, thick dust on the windowsills and skirting boards, muddying the base of the curtain. Perhaps this is where the other man lives. At the very end of the balcony, there are external stairs leading to the service road, but the stairs are blocked with fence wire, barbed wire at the top, coiled in perfect symmetrical loops. Heading back to the two-day room, Clare discards the large bag, clutches her handbag to her chest and looks around for an answer. With her hand in the pocket of her jeans, she clutches her hip and pleads Cliff's name. Then she says: *Shutup—Shutup. Stupid cunt.* She crawls along the verandah, fearing Jem is watching from the water. Where is he? Where is the other man—the creepshow man with the hairy hands?

She chooses the far corner of the verandah, at the opposite end to the padlock and the barbed wire. At this end, the verandah is sheltered by an enormous Moreton Bay Fig. She considers tying the blanket to the railing or the fretwork so she can lever down but mohair is so fibrous. It will never hold her. Anyway, she doesn't want to flag her departure with a yellow blanket. She climbs the railing, edging herself over, taking hold of the timber first and then shifting down the iron fretwork, one hand at a time, like monkey-bars, legs dangling. She's not strong enough to hold her own hanging weight, as heavy as two large men. Where are they? She thinks of Jem's shoulders, surfer triceps, squared-off biceps—she pictures the smirking loiterer with the enormous hands, olive mounds for knuckles. She drops to the gravel. Her thigh and buttock hit the earth first, then her shoulder, saving her head from thumping too hard. Lying there, her leg spasms a short while. She tries to get up. Standing, groaning, adjusting her bag over her panging shoulder, she cries rhythmically and unashamedly, taking a few higgledy steps. She wets her pants in abrupt squirts. She is not a pants-wetter. Is it blood? Why would she be bleeding so violently? She can walk but only just—awkward and buckled. After a time, she limps faster, crying freely now, hobbling hopelessly to the servo, huddling near the drinks fridge to call a cab.

On the way home, she googles *medullary*. It is a real word. It means: relating to the medulla. It can be about any part of the body, any organ. It means: resembling bone marrow.

Along the highway, she peels off her coat, vomits into the hood. *AY!* Says the driver, pulling over. *What the hell?*

There's no mess, she says. *I caught everything in my coat. I'm okay. I'm fine*, she says. *Keep driving. I'll pay more. I'll pay whatever. I'm good now. Sorry. I have a headache. I fell off...*

She folds the hood into the body of the coat, rolls the vomit tight like a towel and holds it in her lap. She can taste fresh blood on her lip. She turns to the sea, thinking of the drive here, putt-putting along the highway in the Kombi—the van seemed higher than it was wide, shifting left and right along the highway as if Jem were half-cut. Most likely he was. Clare felt as though they were moving forward but, equally, sideways—at the mercy of the wind like spindly gum trees, like all of us.

At home, Clare smashes her phone against the bathtub, one-two-three times. It's unnecessary vandalism—he won't call. There is nothing left to say—they exhausted each other in the two-day room.

Jem must never find her. Is he trying to find her or does he have another two-day woman? Should she call the cops? What to say? *...The two-day room—what is that, exactly? What do you mean it felt dangerous? Was this consensual?*

The intensity was untenable. It felt like love but she's not altogether sure. She's never been desired so ferociously—at the mercy of herself and someone else, all at once. It was mostly awful and yet she couldn't get enough. It was frightening and she's glad to be clear of it, but she also savours the memory of it, treasures it from a distance.

There are only a small number of people in the world who love you so much they want to kill you, she thinks, and then she wants to take it back—shameful woman-hating thought. Perhaps Jem didn't mean to lock her in that room. Maybe it was an accident. Was it really as dark as she remembers? She was free to leave, more or less, and she went there willingly. Maybe it was herself she feared, and she projected that onto him, in part at least.

She contributed to the strangeness. Some of it was her doing. Perhaps if they'd slept a little... They forced each other awake relentlessly—it does strange things to your mind. Maybe it was her fear of what she was when she was with him—the never-enough sense that, somehow, she'd wasted herself in the life she lived—perhaps that's what made him seem dangerous.

It could be that he was only ferociously earnest, and occasionally violent. It's possible she brought that out in him. It's not her fault, of course, she hasn't lost her mind, but it's vexed—maybe she coaxed it, probing him rather than asking herself the questions. Maybe that's it.

Note to self—longing cannot be solved in two-day rooms. Never-again for a clusterfuck-of-a-man.

When they arrived at the two-day room, Clare and Jem stepped out onto the balcony. *Look how far*, said Jem, moving his outstretched arm across the expanse of the sea. Clare placed her hands flat against the timber railing, leaning her body against his torso. He bent his knees into the iron fretwork. *It looks like tomorrow-is-when, as if you can hold forever-ness.*

Clare laughed. It was abstract and slightly nonsensical, almost meaningless, and yet in that moment it was perfectly tactile and crystal clear. She laughed again, resting her head against his chest.

Beyond those first moments, there was not so much laughing. They barely stepped onto the balcony except for the occasional breath of real air, or to cry in peace, and they didn't otherwise leave the room.

In the two-day room there was a lot of crying, quiet happy crying at first, and then messy crying. From the very beginning, it was too much. They knew it was too much and yet they extended the two-day room—they broke the rules from the start and gave themselves longer. There was so much scrutiny—they dissected all of the fragments that brought them to the current version of themselves. If Clare fell asleep, Jem woke her. He had to know—*Why do you say something and then retreat from it? Why the fuck do you fucking do that?* Clare woke him too—they both did it, relentlessly—She said: *Why do you always qualify your memories?* She clutched his hand. There are not many gestures so intimate, even for lovers. She said: *Tell me what you saw. Don't tell me what the other people thought, or what you think they thought. I don't care about them. Give it to me straight.* They fossicked through each other's stories, fucked each other raw, every which way, and tried to piece together what they thought they knew of each other.

In the still dark, the bathroom tap dripped, counting down the time they had left. They woke each other constantly, it was exhausting, but then they were not really asleep, not fully—they were in each other's dreams now. Clare clutched Jem's neck, under his ear. Her hold was too tight. *Wake up*, she said. *Tell me something...* The magpies sang. It sounded like they were calling each other. It was a relief, the emerging daylight and the birds singing, the sunshine smell of the sea on the breeze. Clare sank fast, into something like real sleep. Jem pushed his hand between her thighs, urgent fingers flexed. *Tell me*, he said... *What are you thinking about right now?*

Clare turns the affair over in her mind. Was it an affair? What else to call it? She thinks Jem wanted to kill her. She doesn't think he would have, but she feels he definitely wanted to *end* her if she couldn't give him exactly what he wanted. He held her chin, speaking earnestly: *Can you disappear from your old life?* Everything he said was so intentional. He probably wasn't even aware of his fingers, pegging in at her hip. *Look me in the eye*, he pleaded. *Tell me what you see.* He braced both of her hips, firmly, as if he was on his surfboard, ready to stand and take the wave. He came so close to her face that she thought he was going to kiss her. She could feel the breathy vibration of his words on her lips, her chin. He said: *What do you want, precisely?* She could smell his breath, like camel hair.

Jem's breath was dead—like dirty hay and old excrement. He drank too much. It evened him out, dampened the ferocious intensity, but it was too much. Clare was no teetotaller, not by a long stretch. If anything, she was on the lenient side about how much was too much. Jem pushed it past the point. All the while he was steady with it, seasoned—you'd never know if you didn't know. Being with him felt like a kind of dying, an acute kind of living beside-death. It seemed both limitless and perilous. He made Clare wonder what she was capable of, as if suddenly there was so much wasted potential.

What do you want, precisely? Jem asked, again and again. It seemed a fair enough question—still, she couldn't put her finger on an answer. She thinks he might have asked himself the same question. What did he want, precisely? She thinks that turning the question back on him is a good thing, even now, after the fact—perhaps it will bring her back to herself.

Will it? Tell me now, fractious motherfucker. What were you asking of me?

Clare thinks that, in truth, she and Jem both wanted everything from each other, only neither of them could determine, precisely, what everything was. In the beginning, he played a different version of himself, calm and measured and patient, rather than all-consuming and never-ever satisfied. She shouldn't have woken him up in return, she thought it was a game—mean sex—hands at the back of her neck, all his weight, her face pressed hard against the pillow—smothering, faceless sex—how can you come when I'm crying? Is this rape? I'm shuddering because I'm crying without air—I'm not turned-on by the hurting. I'm not coming. Am I coming? Can I be turned-on and come and be raped and cry and be suffocated? Did I provoke this?

Clare only knows bodily thought. Is there another way to know and understand? *Tell me with your hand-words. Stop. Don't Stop.* Clare can't think outside her body. Is it possible? She doesn't believe it is. Knowing something bodily is a type of truth, she thinks. It may be the only type, she adds, in conversation with herself. She thinks this may be her truest thought, ever.

Clare turns things over and over—this plus this, equals... she has no idea how to live her old life. The world has become groundless. She's a stranger inside her own skin. Is there anything more frightening? *Is there? Answer me with your stiffened fingers.*

Clare no longer adds up and that's fine because she is no longer a woman who thinks adding up is necessarily the way to go. She no longer believes that longing can be managed or love is a choice. She thinks that, even at the best of times, love is frayed and moderately fuckeyed.

She can't make sense of what happened because it doesn't make sense—it never will, and so it's a grief that cannot be overcome. It is carried. Carry on.

Clare thought she could leave all that longing in the two-day room like a bloodied towel.

Stop—You're hurting me—Tell me something.

Clare doesn't shy away from remembering because what's the point? Remembering is relentless like a selfish man. She figures she deserves to re-inhabit the horror of that time—the promise and pretence that what-we-have and what-we want-from-each-other might settle in the tell-me and give-it of a locked-down space, confined time, two days turned to five—half-closed curtains, no real air, time inverted like a dome, sunlight refracting from the mirror like fingers—spread, flexed, lit.

Perhaps, thinks Clare, I am not built for love. How to live without it, though? What else is there?

Answer me now you tiger-eyed motherfucker. Give it. I'm begging.

RENT

by Melissa Lucashenko

For a queasy moment Julie thought that there had been some sort of a shameful mistake. She was prone to thinking this, having grown up in a home where such mistakes were made on a regular basis. Then she realised with relief that the key in her hand needed to turn to the left, not the right. The blue door of the dwelling (*shack* was the word the owner had used on the phone) swung open, and it was real after all.

The plain white room reminded Julie of the times during her marriage when she had had reason to stay in motels. She tried the switch beside the door. The owner was right, the power was off. Gazing around, she marvelled at the blankness. The empty space was like a stretched canvas before the paint is bought, an invitation to dream. It was a very long time since Julie had lived alone – there had been a marriage, three children and then a scattering of grandchildren in turn - and now she found the idea of solitude bemusing. It had taken only two brief emails and a phone call to lead her here, standing inside a virtual stranger's house with the door ajar and the metal key still cool in her hand.

'The fishing shack we just bought is empty,' the owner had said, 'We thought we'd ask if you wanted to look after it, rent-free, for a while. It's on the creek at Old Barrow. We won't be around till winter, and we'll rent a bigger place at first, when we do come back, since we'll need extra room for Lauren until semester begins.'

Julie heard nothing more after 'Old Barrow.' Her mind roared with possibilities, and in three days she was on the Coolangatta plane.

Right away Julie made a rule for herself. Nonsensical, but still. Since the bare room was a gift, she had to furnish it for under a hundred dollars. Then and only then, she could stand on her ancestral land and say: *I came back home and it cost me nothing.* If anybody had asked, she could not have explained her rule; all she knew was that it had somehow to do with dignity.

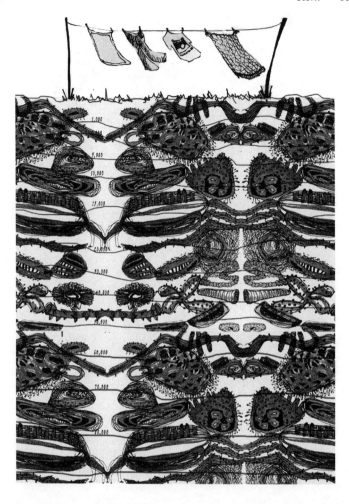

She folded her clothes into the cupboard, then stepped back out onto the red soil of the yard. A handful of sheltering palm trees and the crash of the waves breaking just beyond the carpark told her she had made the right decision. Julie greeted the Ancestors, breathed in a deep lungful of salt air and knew true joy. Discarded oyster shells crunched under her runners when she went to prop the redundant For Sale sign against the garden shed. Then she shut the blue door, climbed into her car and spent the rest of the afternoon across the river.

The second-hand shops in her grandmother's fishing town had gentrified into Old Wares Emporiums, now stocking twenty-dollar colanders, and declarative wooden signs about Love and Family. Sighing as she turned to go, Julie noticed a long-haired eccentric in the community shed beneath the pines. The man had flung a vanload of clothes and crockery onto the wooden picnic tables, along with badly illustrated religious pamphlets. All of it free to everyone, he proclaimed, 'in the spirit of Christmas'.

Driving home with some of his plates and bowls on the front seat, Julie turned things over in her mind. Give and take. Granny hadn't provided a name for this reciprocity, but then they hadn't ever needed a name.

Here, take some eggs when you go, sis. Grandad loved them scones of yours.

I'll drop that pattern around for you when I pick the kids up, Shirl.

Charlie done the floors for me, so I let him have the car for the night.

It was ridiculous, the way the free crockery kept nagging at her as she washed it and put it in the empty cupboard. Life was about give and take, an endless cycle of balancing. Not give and give. And she had enough on her credit card, these days, to go to Kmart for new plates. But the eccentric had merely paused and then gone right on educating her about the local area after she had quietly said *I'm Bundjalung.* So...

Julie imagined telling Pat her qualms. She could hear her sister bray with loud laughter and suggest that she give the man the shirt off her back or the shoes off her feet, if her conscience troubled her over half a dozen plastic bowls. Its Granny's land, Pat added sharply in Julie's imagination, he should be paying us for the privilege of setting up shop. *I know all that*, Julie sighed, *you don't understand*, before heading off to harvest some of the yellow guavas growing on the muddy track beyond the carpark. She gave a wave to the neighbour, who had been mowing his pristine lawn since she arrived.

Julie enjoyed the challenge of her hundred-dollar rule, remembering very well the years when she had no choice about frugality. Fifty dollars at a garage sale bought her a chipped wooden bed. She recycled a red carpet from a skip at the supermarket, along with two perfectly adequate plastic chairs. A borrowed lounge had stiff yellow cushions that needed to be pushed back into place each afternoon. On the third day, when the dwelling looked like someone really lived there, Julie kneeled to assemble a dozen novels in the space built cleverly into the head of the bed. A reader, she knew what Steinbeck had said about the books you had always been meaning to read and never would, but she was determined. In this new house - *shack* was ridiculous, for the place had tiles, and electricity, and hot water, even a bathtub - she would get through those books, and come out the other side, better educated, more thoughtful, wiser. Better equipped to be living here proper way on her grandmother's land.

Pat snorted loudly at that. Need books to live at Old Barrow! You womba? Granny was illiterate, or good as. Write her name, maybe. *She taught us every plant, every tree, some of the Latin names, even,* Julie countered. Books are just another way of knowing.

Have you gorn and seen her, nagged Pat, who came over every week all the way from Ironpot Creek. Sat and yarned with Granny, the family gossip, and talked about the days when Old Barrow was nothing but blackfellers and fishermen. Yarning to the empty air about times long gone, Julie thought, but never said. There were some wounds you just didn't open.

Not yet, she told Pat. Soon.

Julie was woken the following day by next door's mower yammering, but beside the fence this time. And not moving anywhere fast, neither. She swore and heaved herself up. Cranky, she stuck her head above the wooden palings to see Mike collecting fallen palm fronds to add to his pyramid on the verge. Old mate must have oodles of petrol to keep the engine running for nothing like that. More damn money than sense. Ever heard of climate change pal? She went back inside and shut the windows on Mike's side of the house. Flicked the kettle on then laughed at herself. As if Mike'd worry about petrol. He lived in Old Barrow. Millionaire's bloody row, these days.

At the end of the first week Julie found a cardboard carton under the sink, sealed with packing tape so old that its khaki had faded almost to clear. She sliced it open with the tip of a ballpoint pen, a trick remembered from her university night-stacking job. Inside the carton were three dozen cans labelled Aroy-D, Pousses de Bambou. She opened one, sniffed the contents, and tipped the bamboo shoots into a bowl filled from the rainwater tank. Waste not, want not. An old Uncle had told her once how his people up north made bread from cycads.

Soaked the nuts for a long time in the creeks to drain the poison. She resolved to keep changing the water until the nasty tinniness was all gone. This frugality with the food – *taking care* - would be a gesture to the country she was living on.

Thinking of the northern Elder made Julie remember that Granny was still waiting, unvisited. Only, could you call it waiting?

Pat rasped down the phone line.

What's the catch?

No catch. Free for six months, maybe more.

Don't gimme that, there's always a catch. Or do they wanna feel all righteous sharing what they stole, is that it?

Maybe. Wasn't their family what stole it, but.

It's their family hanging onto it.

Look, sis, I wake up hearing the waves, same as when we was littles. There's fish in the creek and rainwater in the tank. Just be happy for me, can't ya?

Any oyster? And what's that noise?

Oh, Mike next door. Forever bloody mowing. There's oyster down the bridge still. Plenty old shell lying around the yard, too. Shred your jinung real quick ya got no shoe.

You wanna get a stick and start digging, sis. That shell might go eight foot down.

A thrill ran between the women at the idea.

Claim it, Pat said cheekily. Claim it onetime.

Can't claim private land. And they're my friends, ay.

Heritage mob, then. Slap an order over it. Keep the developers away at least.

Julie laughed. When she thought about middens and Heritage Orders she saw her six months leave-without-pay twisting and buckling into endless complications. It was easier to laugh.

I'll bring it back this arvo, Julie told Mike from behind the steering wheel. Be real good to have the place tidied up, ay. She looked across at her red-dirt yard of tufted grass and oyster shell. A stray palm frond lay under the clothesline. In Mike's eyes, Bedlam.

Keep the blades on number three, Mike told her, slapping the mower's yellow bonnet. Up and out of trouble. Julie slipped the earmuffs down into place and revved the engine. Gave him the thumbs up.

Will do, boss.

Ya went and seen her, then. About time. Pat was sitting on the plastic chair from the skip, nursing a joint. How she'd gotten inside the house, Julie had no idea.

Yeah. Her face tight with not saying more to her big sister. About the joint, the locked house. About the shock of Granny, lying there with the lights on but nobody home.

Ya coulda warned me, Julie muttered. Her arms hung slack, her strength drained by a scrap of an old dark woman lying prone in the Home. The nothingness of her, who had climbed sand dunes with four-year old Julie swaying on her shoulders.

Don't judge a book by its cover, sis. She's in there.

I couldn't stand it. Julie meant this literally. Her legs had gone to jelly.

Ah, Gran knows who comes to visit her. Ask that dialysis nurse with the scars, Brenda. She'll tell ya straight up

Uh-huh. Julie had no intention of ever going back to the Home.

Gran and Brenda had a proper long yarn once. There was this show on about the '73 cyclone. Biggest yarn bout the old days, Brenda reckons. That was before Uncle John went, mind, and she's kept pretty schtum ever since. But the Old Girl's in there alright.

I can't stand it, Julie repeated hopelessly. Seeing her pitiful like that.

Pat stared, affronted.

You better start to stand it then. That Old Girl needs to come home. Now you've got this place-. The joint in her right hand described the logic of this assertion, arcing between cause and effect.

She needs round-the-clock care, Julie choked.

And so? We care for her, then. Sis, it's Old Barrow.

It'd kill her.

She's dying anyway.

Julie lifted her head from her novel. The day's blissful silence had been interrupted. Mike along with the bloke from Beachside Mowing and Maintenance, manhandling the ride-on mower up onto a trailer. Straining and yelling as they heaved.

Good luck with that. Julie eyed the starter motor resting on the kitchen bench.

How's it all going? The Owner asked. Are you getting a lot of work done?

Yes, she said. Pat felt like a lot of work. Always had.

We've decided we're moving up at Easter, the Owner added brightly. But don't worry, we won't knock the shack down till much later. The building approval has to go through first.

Oh, said Julie, with a familiar heavy feeling settling upon her chest. Oh, the building approval. Okay.

After, she threw her phone on the bed and grabbed a bread knife from the cupboard. Stood at the open door for a long minute, sunk in thought. Then squatted by the clothesline and started to dig.

We're all going on a summer holiday, Pat sang in triumph as she zipped shut a small suitcase. Hey Gran? We're all going where the sea is blue.

Half your luck, said Nurse Brenda, reaching down with muscular pink-scarred arms. On the count of three. Between them the women lifted Granny, surprisingly heavy for the mere scrap that she was, onto the hospital trolley. Her brown eyes, cloudy with cataracts, wandered as they wheeled her away from the dementia ward.

This is the lift, Gran, Pat told her. This is the lobby. This is the carpark, now. You've effected your escape, Old Girl, we're bustin ya out. This is ya seatbelt. Gotta make sure ya get home safe n sound to country, ay.

Pat swore that Gran grinned, but Julie had missed it.

Installed in the front seat, the old grey head lolled a little. Lie her back a bit, instructed Nurse Brenda as she wiped a faint trickle of saliva from Gran's chin. Julie bent over to press the lever and ease Gran's seat back on an angle. For a moment the old eyes seemed to gaze right into her own and brighten; Julie caught a sharp breath. But when she stood to go around to the driver's side, Gran continued looking in exactly the same way, in the same direction, at the tall buildings lining the nearby streets. It didn't matter to Gran that she wasn't there. *What the hell are we doing?* Julie thought, in sudden silent fury. *Who is this charade even for?*

Pat wanted the Golden Oldies on, and so it was Perry Como and Nat King Cole for forty kays down the highway, along with remember this spot Gran, this is where we went fishing with Uncle John that time and Sam stepped on the bullrout, didn't he bloody yell, ay, oh, and here's where the frozen banana stall used to be, and do you remember the lovely big draft horses that used to be in this paddock, do you remember...

Do you remember, Gran, when you were little, when they took you away? Remember coming home to Uncle John and your brothers and sisters scattered to the winds? Or years later in Ballina, when your brain went wrong and you never spoke sense again? Remember that time an hour ago when we got you released from the hospital to take you home one last time and you were a fucking vegetable instead of a human being, do you remember that?

As they peeled off the highway and drove down the dirt road leading into Old Barrow Julie began to weep with rage. Shut up, will you, she told Pat. Just shut up. She wrenched savagely at the steering wheel and brought the car to a skidding halt on the side of the track. Red dust flew up, coating everything in sight. She turned the engine off and turned to her sister in the back.

She doesn't fucking remember anything, Julie spat. This is all about *you*, not about her.

When her accusations were spent, and Pat's own harsh truths had been flung back in return, and the sisters had finished their raging, Julie leaned forward. She rested her head against the steering wheel and keened. A great shudder of exhaustion passed through her. What's gone is gone, and there's no use pretending. No use looking back. She straightened, her decision made.

Ring the Home, she told Pat. You can tell them she's coming back. And god help you if they don't have a bed for her.

Julie swung the nose of the car into the middle of the road, facing the creek, then slammed the car into reverse. Granny's torso tipped forward. As she lurched, the old woman cried out wordlessly, and reached a papery hand onto the dash.

Jesus! Can you bloody settle down?!! Pat leaned in from the back, steadying Gran with a savage look at her sister. Julie put the car in neutral, smacked the volume button hard, silencing Ella Fitzgerald.

You're the one wanted to bring her here, genius. I said it'd be too much for her, but nah-

We *owe her*, don't you get that? We owe it to her to at least try!

Julie breathed out a long, exasperated sigh as Pat carefully rearranged Gran. Hauled her back into position as gently as she could, while her head lolled and her dark wrinkled fingers trailed limply down the dashboard, making five long shining rivers appear in the coating of dust. That'd be right. Steal a country just to ruin it. Rivers all over the place turned to dry red powder. Ashes to ashes. Paradise to dust.

Upright again in her seat, Granny turned her right hand over in her lap, gazed blankly down at the dusted dark fingertips. The red and the black, thought Julie, glancing over as she put the car into gear, the red and the black. A bit like the flag. Or poppies.

We tried, she thought. Nobody can say we didn't try.

Hold still now, Old Girl, Pat said gently from the rear. Julie reached for the radio knob, ready again for Ella Fitzgerald, and Gran mimicked her, reached forward again too, touching the dash with one shaking finger.

My country, she whispered. *My country.*

RAGTIME IN EDEN

by Roger Vickery and Ian Hood

Cards at sea were jazz for us. We were a slick combo, honed by scores of nights in rocking cabins, to take the piss with coded ease.

Got two hearts.

Bastard. Two hearts?

And a seven! God swallow-me-elbow.

Are you out-outy-out?

Aaah! Left the bower have they?

Mutton played aggro runs with double bass intensity. *In your arse with 42 brooms...Where'd that fuckin king come from?*

Slapsy was our drummer, kept time and rhythm, sliding into soothing brush work whenever Mutton plucked too hard. *Seems to be moderatin'. Bit like yesterday. Moderated, then blew away like a gypsy's promise.*

I was baritone sax, partial to a showy verbal lick if a winning hand found its way to my bower. One night, joker and trump suit in fist, I announced in my best Barry White voice: no man will be a sailor who has contrivance enough to get himself into gaol. *A man there has more room, better food and company and little chance of being drowned.*

Slapsy smiled and nodded.

Mutton belched. *Who said that...Captain Fuckin Arab?*

Doctor Samuel Johnson, I drawled. Knew a thing or two about the sea, the good doc did. Joker and Jack. Read 'em and grow lachrymose.

Tall and gangly, hair down to his shoulders, giggle hat two sizes large, rode a 250cc Virago, the loser's Harley...Tobee never fitted on the boat.

First day as a deckie, keener than a hungry gull to be liked, he answered to: *Hairy legs...hey spider... pelican shit...pea-head.*

Met every insult with a grin.

Chugging back into Eden, our skipper, near broke, tic in his right eye fluttering like a hooked gill, ordered us to the stern:

I need crew. No funny stuff, boys. Least not while the mackerel's running.

I had a kid somewhere down south, close to Tobee's age. Did my best to throw a net over the crew whenever the boy crossed the line. But the silly mongrel lacked the legs for boat or land.

In the back bar of the Australasia Hotel, three Tooheys' Olds aboard, he'd list and sway, giggle when he should've grinned, yell when a semaphore shrug was needed and open his mouth like a stranded groper if a hard arse offered him a knuckle sandwich.

Mutton, Slapsy and me would swear and side arm through the crowd, schooners held high. Grim as greenies protecting a baby seal, we'd hip nudge that night's Jimmy Sharman clear of his prey until Tobee could turn rudder and bolt for the boat. Sometimes our groyne work stirred up a storm and we had to bash and bail our way into Imlay Street.

Crews stick in Eden.

We were rocking at anchor in Twofold Bay when I duplicated my Joker and Jack trump trick. Slapsy gave me a finger. Mutton grabbed his crutch. I grinned like a riverboat gambler and lunged across the gimbal table to claim my pile.

But Tobee had a tin ear. Instead of ragtime he heard ACDC bagpipes.

Eager to join the bigger battalion he yelped *cheat, fuckin cheat* he scattered my cards and crossed our line for good.

One week later, moored off Eden, skipper safely rubber-duckied into town, we turned *Walking the Dog* on full blast and tied a rope around Tobee's waist. The boy was laughing until Mutton clipped him over the ears. I assured him everything would be okay and ruffled his hair as we lowered him over the side.

Our plan was two times around the boat, giving him a message, three parts joking, one part plain -- *Time to move on, little doggie.*

The rope went slack around the starboard stay.

We freed the dinghy in record time. Mutton dived and came up with the goods. The boy groaned. That gave us hope. Slapsy worked his chest. I did mouth. Thirty compressions, two breaths. Thirty compressions, two breaths. We pumped and kissed him for an age.

The coroner bought our story he must have tumbled overboard while taking a piss.

The town knew different and marked our cards.

We're finished on boats around here. No point in protesting. We know the rules.

Crews stick in Eden.

GOSPEL FOR A BLACK JESUS

by Graham Sheil

When the Pacific War ended, the Australian Minister of External Territories flew to Port Moresby to receive the salute at a ceremonial march past. The ceremony culminated in the Honourable Edward Ward decorating a number of serving officers and men, including a north coast New Guinea man. He and an Australian officer escaped Rabaul when Australian forces surrendered and the two later escaped the island of New Britain. He then led small contingents of local and Australian troops on attack-and-disappear missions against an increasingly hungry and dispirited enemy.

The formal citation read out by Minister Ward told of the man's exemplary ability to lead men in situations where there was no possibility of relief or reinforcement and the contingent had to rely on the jungle and local villagers for sustenance.

Having read out the formal citation, the Minister - notorious for being a firebrand orator, labelled 'Red Eddie' by an antagonistic press - permitted himself an observation of gentle whimsy.

'With that name of "Moses" it's no wonder you were able to *lead your people* in war, as, I have no doubt, you will in peace.'

The name 'Moses' had been bestowed when a missionary inflated the tally of his converts by subjecting an entire village to full-immersion baptism that washed away *wantok* (clan) names and substituted Biblical names.

As for Moses *leading his people*, that proved to be more difficult in peace than in war. In the exigencies of jungle warfare, illiteracy had been no impediment; but the performance of peacetime duties required by his rank placed Moses in the humiliating position of having written, directives, requisitions, orders, read to him. Then there was the law which limited social interaction with Australians of his rank.

Once he had gone into an officers' wet mess. The barman came around the bar to the other side and asked Moses to accompany him to the foyer.

'I know who you are, Sir. I know men who served under you. Believe me, I'd be *proud* to drink with you. But to serve you, Sir, would cost me my job.'

Just then Carruthers, *Major* Carruthers, strode into the foyer.

He did not address Moses, but spoke past Moses to the barman.

'What's he doing here?'

'He *fought* in the war!'

The barman's intonation betraying the contempt men who fought in the jungle felt toward those they saw as having spent the war as desk-bound bum-shiners.

He remembered to add, 'Sir,' before beginning to recite what he knew of Moses' war record.

Major Carruthers interrupted, 'Escaped New Britain, eh?'

'With MacCreadie, Sir. District Administrator MacCreadie, as he is now.'

'I *know* who MacCreadie is! If you listen to that blowhard you'll hear how he won the war on his own!'

The barman knew he was on dangerous ground but persisted.

'Moses, Sir, he's been decorated. The Minister for External Territories presented and pinned on his colour -

'I can *see* his colour! Get that boong out of here!'

Moses got himself eased out of the army. He returned to his north coast village where he was hailed as a war hero, became an important man in *wantok* affairs and known for his oratory, the great art of New Guinea men.

Among fellow officers and civilian expatriates Alexis MacCreadie was renowned as a raconteur. He would tell with gusto how he and Moses burgled a munitions shed and blew up a wharf. He told of pursuit, of near capture and near death, his account culminating in the construction of a platform to join two local canoes and a sail from *pit-pit* (split bamboo) matting for the sea voyage from New Britain.

Those regaled by MacCreadie might well have suspected him of sacrificing accuracy for impact, yet there can be no doubting the efficacy of his telling: it had been his account of escape and sabotage that ensured Moses' role was formally recognized and began his rise through the ranks.

Before the war, MacCreadie had been a *kiap* (Australian patrol officer). After escaping New Britain his weapons of war became binoculars and a radio; his defence, the ability to gain the trust of local people.

After the end of hostilities, MacCreadie was appointed District Administrator over the same north coast province he had patrolled as a kiap and from where he reported by radio on the movements of enemy planes and ships and troops from within enemy territory.

This was the same province to which Moses returned.

District Administrator MacCreadie's residence was two blocks from the centre of the town with its mission-owned and shipping company-owned trade stores, export and shipping agency offices, a Chinese emporium and the town *bung* (market). His home was an unrelieved rectangle on stilts with a veranda beneath which he parked his jeep.

He had settled himself on his veranda for his evening tipple, when town dogs announced the approach of a visitor on foot.

Although no longer in the army, when Moses visited MacCreadie he wore boots highly polished, long khaki trousers, khaki shirt with epaulettes, a webbing belt buckled at the precise centre of his bearing. By the time Moses stepped from the top step onto the veranda, MacCreadie had already splashed dark liquid from a square bottle into the glass he held out to his visitor. The District Administrator spanned with a joke the chasm between the law he was charged to administer and the crime he was at that moment enacting. A *very* MacCreadie joke.

'Tell y' what, Mate - longer you wear that uniform, whiter you look.'

The two former comrades in arms were in cane chairs on MacCreadie's veranda, drinking rum, when Moses related a *stori* (story with traditional and mythic elements) being relayed from village to village. This *stori* gave explanation for the great revelation the war had conferred on villagers: people of distant lands had an unlimited abundance of material goods, goods that they - *rabis pipal bilong Nuigini* (rubbish people of New Guinea) - did not possess. In this tale all the cargo local people had ever seen unloaded from ships or disgorged from planes was made in Japan. When Japanese people learnt people *bilong Nuigini* had not their abundance of cargo, *they sorri in their hearts for rabis pipal bilong Nuigini* and put trucks and generators, outboard motors and electric light, tinned mackerel and Bundaberg rum, shot guns, electric torches - all cargo! - into ships and planes to deliver to people *bilong Nugini.*

MacCreadie guessed where this *stori* was going.

'Only those ships and planes didn't get here - right?'

'Right, Alex. Right! Australians they no want New Guinea people they get cargo.

Australian soldiers they shoot down planes. They sink ships.'

'So *that's* why we fought the war!' MacCreadie whooped. 'I was wondering.'

He really was wondering - about the effect this *stori* would have upon village audiences. When MacCreadie's life depended upon seeing the world through the eyes of local people, he had come to comprehend that for them nothing was wholly real unless it was encapsulated within *stori.* MacCreadie had his own project to lift local people out from their perception of themselves as a rubbish people.

'What about it, Mate? What about putting your oratory to good use - convincing villagers to start their own plantations?'

There'd be more to it than convincing villagers to burn scrub, clear jungle, till the ground, pool money and goods of exchange for seeds, germinate seeds in nursery gardens, plant out seedlings. Plantation produce had to find markets. Villagers weren't ready to do that on their own. They'd need the co-operation of expat companies. The last thing he needed was to have antagonism between expats and locals set in *stori.*

'What about it, eh?- You can tell villagers a better *stori* than that one.'

This was not the first time MacCreadie had attempted to enlist his one-time comrade in arms to be front man for his project.

Moses set his glass down onto the floor and he stepped to the veranda rail. During the war he'd commanded Australian and local troops, since the war he could not even lawfully drink with men he'd commanded. From the rail he looked out over village houses of *pit-pit* matting and pandanus thatch to a beach of broken coral and a lagoon that reached to a line of breakers.

'What about it? Your oratory and your reputation as a war hero will bring people flocking to hear you. They'll listen - *really* listen - to you.'

That *stori*, MacCreadie was thinking, could wreck his project before it began. And doing nothing was, as local people said, a *nambawan* (number one) way to ensure people who had come to see themselves as *rabis pipal* STAYED *rabis pipal!*

'S'pose white-skin he do this work?'

' He'd be paid.' MacCreadie cut him off. 'Too right he would! And you will too.'

'Paid?'

'You'll be paid - *all-same kiap.*'

'All-same kiap ?'

MacCreadie knew well , too well! , *kiaps* constantly grumbled about their rates of pay and their formal position within the Administration. They had their own expression for that, *Lower than shark shit*. But among villages to which patrols took them, there they were the Administration. They had their own expression for that, too, *God's shadow on earth*.

'All-same kiap, Mate. All-same.'

MacCreadie had neither the authority to make that offer nor the budget to implement it. Yet he saw at one stroke he could restore to Moses that sense of self-worth he possessed when he commanded troops. Well, he'd subject his meagre budget to creative accounting. It wouldn't be the first time.

He picked up Moses' glass from the veranda planking, poured in more rum, took it and his own glass to where Moses stood at the veranda rail. He handed Moses his glass and raised his own.

'God's shadow on earth, Mate. God's shadow on earth.'

Over two-way radio, MacCreadie followed Moses' progress in exhorting villagers along the north coast and inland as far as foothills to the highlands. Accounts he received came from *kiaps* on patrol, from prospecting expeditions, mining camps, distant missions and trade stores. Moses' oratory fuelled the aspiration of people to lift themselves out of their perception of themselves as a rubbish people. They cleared jungle, obtained, nurtured, planted out, seedlings of coconut and oil palm, coffee and tea bushes, vanilla orchids.

MacCreadie's satisfaction at Moses igniting so much hope-inspired effort was tempered by wondering how long that flame could be kept burning. How long until coffee bushes were ready for picking? Five years, was it? Six? How long before oil palms were ripe for harvest?

Coconut palms produce copra? The time before tea leaves took on the glossy tinge that signalled they were ready to be picked?

MacCreadie was not the only one to harbour doubts. When he encountered a plantation or mine manager in the streets of the town, at the *bung* or the expatriates' club, he would be greeted with backslapping bonhomie, though soon the conversation would turn to proclaim the perceived consequences of his project. Wages would rise, profits fall, investments dwindle.

MacCreadie could be an imposing presence. Short and stocky, habitually wearing shorts and long socks worn short, rolled onto boot-tops, legs muscular from years of patrolling as a *kiap*, he had a way of standing as if he confronted a tidal wave. Those who put criticism to him would baldly state their case before recollecting a matter of immense importance and urgency and hurry away.

Criticism of another kind came from missions. Since the war, the established missions - Catholic and Lutheran and Seventh Day Adventists - had to compete with missions of denominations previously unknown. As MacCreadie saw it, he had to waste time,- too much time!- adjudicating disputes between missions. So, he was surprised to receive over two-way radio the request that he receive a deputation from combined missions.

When the delegation arrived, among them was Pat Keane. He was a Catholic missionary priest who had come to New Guinea filled with evangelical fervour that drained from him as he embraced this land and its people. He had become a sometime tippling companion of MacCreadie. Pat Keane stepped onto the veranda ahead of the others.

MacCreadie said, 'Didn't expect to see you among this lot.'

'I'm mystified myself,' Pat Keane said. 'All I know, I was invited.

When the rest of the delegation reached the veranda and moved inside, there was talk of a boat that docked the previous evening bringing supplies for which most had been waiting. When that subject was talked to exhaustion, Henderson (Church of England) separated himself from the others.

'Good of you to receive us, Alex.' Henderson said, '*Very* good. We had a prior meeting at which it was decided I act as spokesman. It was decided, unanimously I might say, that you, Alex, are in a far better position than any of us to deal with the present crisis.

MacCreadie glanced at Pat Keane who answered by raising his eyebrows.

'Yes?'

'We, all of us, are experiencing villagers abandoning their missions'.

MacCreadie knew the ache of villagers to regain their sense of self-worth impelled many to flock to newer missions that promised all God's Blessings shall be given unto those who gave themselves to Lord Jesus. When villagers discovered God's Blessings did not extend to a petrol generator, electric light, a jeep, shotgun, marine outboard motor, nor did it include tinned mackerel, Bundaberg rum or bags of rice, those missions too experienced defections.

'Disappointing, no doubt,' MacCreadie said. 'Though hardly a "crisis".'

'Now there's a *stori* going around that the Second Coming is at hand and when Jesus returns He will come as a black man.'

'That began before the war,' MacCreadie said. 'It's persisted because it has a certain logic: white-skins have their white Jesus which is why they have power over people with black skin and access to all manner of loot. So, what *they* need is their own Jesus - a black Jesus - to empower them and deliver them their own cornucopia of cargo.'

The missionaries looked at each other. They seemed disconcerted by the District Administrator's uncompromising account.

Seeing that, MacCreadie added, 'There's actually a good chance, albeit by a different route, villagers will get more than *loaves and fishes*. Good chance they'll take delivery of a petrol generator, a village truck, an outboard motor.'

Henderson visibly steeled himself to resume his role as spokesman.

'Alex, I think we're all aware what you're attempting to put in place, and I think I can say, we're all more-or-less supportive. But I remind you the Administration recognises the…. the… *necessity*.. of missions' -

MacCreadie interrupted, 'Yes, yes.'

He didn't need to be told. This wasn't Australia: if missions didn't provide medical aid and schooling, no one else would. And villagers for-sure needed that. If ever they were going to step into the 20th century, villagers needed all that and more.

'You were saying *I'm* in a position to enact ... whatever it is you've decided.'

Henderson said, 'We had a good look at Papua and New Guinea Statutes of Law.

'Statutes of Law?'

MacCreadie was trying to guess where this was going.

Henderson, as ever reasonable, said, 'There does seem to be one that suits this situation.'

'I'm waiting to hear.'

Now the delegation had got to the point of why they had come, no one seemed to want to be the one who said it.

'Out with it, gentlemen.'

Forester (Evangelical) was the one not able to contain himself, 'Plainly, that law which proscribes Spreading False Rumour.'

'False Rumour?'

'Spreading False Rumour,' said Forester, brightly, 'That seems to fit the bill.'

"Fit the bill"? ... Fits ... the ... bloody ... bill!'

'Al-ex!'

Pat Keane gave a warning shake of his head, but now MacCreadie was launched, he wasn't going to stop. Perhaps he wasn't able to stop.

'You expect me to *kalabus* (jail) villagers for Spreading False Rumour while you lot go 'round promising Heaven, threatening Hell, offering Everlasting Life.

Pat Keane put his head down and turned away.

' - and *they're* to be *kalabused* for Spreading False Rumour!'

There was more talk, much more, but that effectively ended it. When the rest trooped out onto the veranda and down steps, Pat Keane stayed. MacCreadie returned from seeing off the delegation to find Keane sitting on a chair with his head in his hands.

'*Now* we know why you got invited,' MacCreadie said. 'To exert a soothing influence.'

'Most *had* met you before!'

'Can't say you were a great success.'

'Alex, you could have handled that better.'

'Oh? You'd have me *kalabus* villagers for a *stori* that's no more *false rumour* than the one they're pronouncing from pulpits? Or have you, f' Chrissake, recidivated back to when you wore vestments and a dog collar?'

'Not, Alex, not for "*Christ's* sake". For the sake of people we're both trying to lift up to stand on their own two feet when the twenty first century dumps down on them like Niagara. And it will, Alex. It will.'

'F' once we're in agreement. Keep that up and we'll have nothing to talk about.'

'While you're being so agreeable ... see if we can agree on this: *that lot*, as you call them, aren't going to just lie down. They came to you for help and you sent them packing. Do you think they'll just slink away? ... Eh? ... Give up? Is that what you think? Or has it occurred to you some of them just might take action of their own?'

'Don't see what action they *can* take.'

'At this moment, I don't either. But I'm damned sure some will, Alex. Some will.'

What that action came to be MacCreadie learnt while moving within the current of news and rumour that never ran dry, the town *bung*. He heard what was being *storied* in villages and what was being pronounced from pulpits. Oh, he knew what missions proclaimed was intended as a rhetorical device against which local people had no defence: rhetorical, no more than that. But MacCreadie's life had depended upon seeing the world through the eyes of local people, and he well knew what was said and how those same words were received could be different. Very different.

What MacCreadie extrapolated from what he heard sent him driving the coast road in pre-dawn dark. Daylight arrived before he reached the village where Moses lived. He roused his one-time comrade-in-arms and they drove the coast road which in places was no more than wheel tracks through sand and in places had the hard compacted surface of crushed coral.

The sun was high in the sky when MacCreadie stopped the jeep where there was a precipitous drop to the sea. Below them, men had built a wharf. That was another manifestation of the hope that possessed villagers and had its basis in their observation of ships and of birds. Ships that disgorged cargo were drawn to deep water wharfs, just as female bower birds were drawn to a male bird's bower.

Moses was wearing his polished boots and his uniform, his belt buckled and the two stood listening to the crash of waves against the cliff and looking down at remnants of the wrecked wharf. MacCreadie had been deliberate in choosing this place where futility was manifest in smashed planks and dislodged pylons strewn among rocks.

MacCreadie broke the silence.

'You know better than me - villagers are working themselves into a frenzy in their hope for a Black Jesus. And they've settled on you, Moses - *you're* their Black Jesus.'

Moses continued to stare into the pitiless glare of sunlight off sea.

'If there was the least truth in this Black Jesus caper, you'd get my vote. You for-sure would. There's just one problem: it's all fantasy, Moses: *nambawan bullshit!*'

Minutes passed before Moses spoke.

'How I know?'

'For Chrissake, Mate - what're you on about?'

'How I know I the Black Jesus?'

Perhaps a minute passed before MacCreadie responded. That villagers wanted to bestow divinity upon Moses was just part of the problem. There would be the expectation they wouldn't need to put in all that work and wait five years or six before their boat came in. That would all happen without effort. By miracle.

'I don't know, Mate. But I reckon if you were you wouldn't be asking me -you'd *know!*'

An enigmatic half-smile appeared on Moses' face as he continued to stare into the distance.

'They'll kill you, Moses , you know that, don't you?' MacCreadie said quietly. 'They'll kill you for-sure.'

Only one way by which the True Jesus can be known, that He rise from the dead: that was what MacCreadie heard at the bung: that pulpit proclamation repeated and repeated.

Moses looked into MacCreadie's face. Then he looked toward where tops of pylons still showed above waves. Men had died, constructing that wharf. Hope, though: hope had not died.

MacCreadie heard himself cry out, 'They'll bloody kill you!'

Still Moses did not respond.

MacCreadie abruptly stepped away from Moses and the edge of the cliff.

'*Jeee-zus*, Moses!'

As abruptly as he started, he stopped. Had he added confusion by his conjunction of Moses with Jesus? And then, was *he* confusing Moses' people with a people of such pride *they* proclaimed themselves the Chosen People? The Roman Empire conquered them and they must have seen themselves as having been diminished. Some among them had been tempted to regain their sense of self-worth by heaping all of their hopes on one of their own. They had bowed down before him and spread palm leaves at his feet. And he, He had been unable to resist the divinity heaped upon Him. For MacCreadie, that was the gut-wrenching human pathos of the Gospels. That's what got Him killed.

'S'pose people they kill me.' Moses was quite matter of fact. 'Next- I know.'

Next?

Next!

MacCreadie dropped to his knees.

'It won't happen, Mate. It just won't bloody happen!'

MacCreadie had given Moses a vision of himself as one who would lead his people to the promised land of village plantations and restoration of their sense of worth. He had bestowed upon Moses that pride possessed by those who pronounced themselves, however jokingly, to be *God's shadow on earth*. But villagers ached to heap upon their war hero not the shadow of divinity but its substance.

Moses came from the edge of the cliff and he spoke so gently his intent could only be to comfort the anguished MacCreadie.

'Next ... I know.'

The news trickled to Pat Keane before it flowed on to flood that river of news and rumour, the town *bung*. What was heard by the man villages still thought of as their priest, sent him driving his dented and inexpertly panel-beaten Ford utility to the town and to MacCreadie.

In Pat Keane's ute they travelled the coast road before turning inland and turn and turn again among foothills to the highlands until they reached the place. Banks of a stream were squeezed between steep jungle slopes and along the wider bank were newly excavated cooking pits, washed stones, piles of firewood, stacked banana leaves, sweet potatoes and taro and plantains, a long line of pigs tethered to stakes.

They walked beyond these preparations for a celebratory feast. Their steps brought them to where the river cut into the base of a cliff on one side and on the other opened out into a wide river flat. Here were people. A multitude of people. Some stood in inward facing groups. Most were seated upon the ground. All were waiting.

And there lay Moses. There were palm leaves at his feet and he was dressed in a woven waistband, *tapa* apron, legs and feet bare, chest naked, a headdress of cuscus fur decorated with quills of cassowary and feathers of bird of paradise, clay-white and starkly yellow designs painted on limbs and chest. Not the traditional dress of his own or any other clan, but a fantastic amalgam of many. His throat was slit.

MacCreadie questioned people of one group and another. All agreed Moses had offered his throat to the blade. As to who swung the blade to the waiting throat, MacCreadie did not ask. That determination could wait.

Pat Keane spread over the body a blanket he had brought. Apostate priest and District Administrator sat on the earth to wait like all the others.

MacCreadie recalled after he and Moses sabotaged a wharf and were being hunted the length of New Britain, they had been surprised on an open beach by a plane that dived and strafed. They ran to put palm trunks between them and guns spitting death. The plane climbed, turned and dived, not to again strafe but release a bomb. MacCreadie was buried. Moses dug him out with bare hands. MacCreadie was unable to stand, unable to eat. He urged Moses to go on without him, but Moses brought him a woman and he sucked milk from her breasts. In his hallucinatory state and even when he knew he would live, it seemed to him he had been restored to life by the ample breasts of this land.

Beside the stream, all waited. They waited through that day and a night and another day. The one-time priest and the District Administrator sustained themselves, as did all the others, not with food brought for their celebratory feast but by chewing on sugarcane, sucking down the sweetness and spitting out the pith.

On the morning of the third day, Pat Keane removed the blanket. Moses did not rise from the dead. What did rise, powerfully, was the stench of putrefaction.

Then all knew there would be no great feast of celebration. People took their sweet potatoes and taro and plantains, their firewood and pigs and they returned to their villages and to lives bereft of their immense hope.

The body was taken to the beach of broken coral below where MacCreadie lived and he and the apostate priest constructed a funeral pyre. Pat Keane put on vestments. As the body burned, he intoned the prescribed verses and prayers for the dead, formalities he performed less for the dead than for the living. MacCreadie had need of such salve as was in his power to administer, these sacraments.

MacCreadie waded into the lagoon to where there was a break in the reef, and he spread the ashes where they would be carried out into the Bismark Sea. At the eastern extremity of that sea, he and Moses had lain for days and nights on a platform joining the two canoes that carried them from New Britain.

That night, Pat Keane took off his vestments to sit in shorts and singlet on MacCreadie's veranda. He had intoned verses that celebrated a miracle he no longer considered actually happened and had offered up prayers to a god in whom he no longer believed. He had no regret. He well knew historic veracity was one thing, the efficacy of sacraments quite another.

When MacCreadie brought out onto the veranda a square bottle and glasses, the apostate surprised the District Administrator by pronouncing that other Jesus had risen from the dead. Oh, not in life. Yet He had, emphatically, risen. He had risen in story.

Next day MacCreadie drove to villages. He questioned. Determined. Arrested. Sentenced and *kalabused*.

He had written any number of reports and the report he wrote was like all the others, it adhered to Administration Guidelines he set down no more than bare facts.

This time, though, the matter was not concluded. In a sense, it had not yet begun.

On some future occasion he would stand glass-in-hand among expatriates, deliberately adopting that intimidating stance of his and he would put the flesh of story on the bare bones of fact. But he foresaw occasions of greater significance. He foresaw himself delivering his tale to those most in need of his telling. He would be seated upon the ground, the night warm and heavy with the smells of the jungle, smell of decomposition and regeneration. Women would be seated upon the ground, giving breast to *pikininis*; men in their tight *wantok* groups, sharing betel-nut. The warm custardy jungle smell would be overlaid by the cloying smell of betel-nut mixed with crushed lime and saliva. Out of courtesy someone would put into his hands a bamboo tube filled with creek-water that had the residual tang of pig shit. He would sip and not be repelled by the taste. He would lift up his head to pitch his voice over villagers, over the *pit-pit* matting and pandanus thatch houses, over pig pens, over gardens with mounds for sweet potato cultivation and channels in which villagers grew taro, his voice reaching into the jungle with its living imperative of putrefaction and rebirth.

By exactly how much such telling would extend beyond the bare facts, he was at that moment uncertain, though much would be added; people bereft of their immense hope had need of the sacrament they called *stori*. He did know, already, how he would begin.

'When the Pacific War ended, the Australian Minister of External Territories flew to Port Morseby to receive the salute at a ceremonial march past. The ceremony culminated in the Honourable Edward Ward decorating a number of serving officers and men, including a north coast New Guinea man ...'

HYMN FOR HOME

by Leslie Thiele

Growing up we lived as nomads. Twelve different schools, six different states, and a few overseas postings thrown in for good measure. Inevitably, at some point in every new school I would find myself standing in the playground in the correct uniform for the school before this one, different, marked out as new. The new kid. The locations and quality of play equipment changed but the routine was depressingly similar.

'Where ya from?'

Standing there, surrounded by avid and dangerous faces, eyes obsidian upon me, I never had an answer which satisfied them or me. I wasn't *from* anywhere and I ached, in the bone deep way only a child can be from *somewhere*. To belong to someplace. Scuffing my shoes on the asphalt, or the dried-out grass, I would stammer out the name of the last town, the last state, the last country. Willing the bell to ring before they became too curious. My face always hot and eyes stinging with unshed tears for those first few torturous weeks while I learned to navigate yet another new group of sceptics.

I know that feeling.

Big shame.

At twenty-five, having never lived anywhere but urban environments, I followed my partner north to the West Kimberley region of Western Australia to live and work on a cattle station. It was supposed to be for one year. It turned instead into twenty two.

New Season

It is impossible to understand 'forever' until you've seen it. It's something about the curve of the earth unfettered, that far horizon. Makes you want to lay your head, just be small, just breathe for a while. It is the reason sailors love the sea, the limitless ocean. All of us, so tiny under a wide canvas of sky, stars, and sunset. The land unfurling toward the petticoat coast and onward across the moody ocean. So much space to traverse until we fetch up somewhere. Learn to just *be*.

The first time I stood on the ground there, some long buried Serengeti DNA rose within me in recognition and respect. The heart of me sank deep and helpless into the ancient dirt and all the coming from, the going to, ceased its thrumming. Something inside lay quiet and satisfied and whole.

Overhead a flock of Brolgas hooted their way across the pink evening sky and landed, already dancing, on the wide plains. They were home and so, somehow, incredibly, was I.

Away from the cities, time takes on a different meaning. Seasons, not clocks, become the marker of our days. The circle of a timepiece begins to mean less than the cycle of the natural world bending around us.

Marrul Season – April

We get the horses ready for the mustering season. They've been turned out in the front paddock since the end of November. Haven't seen a human in five months or more, living like brumbies over the long rumbling wet. Sheltering under Cadjeput stands when the lightning scared them, nose to tail, ceaseless swishing to avoid the mosquitoes and the marsh fly plagues. We round them up with the ute as soon as the paddock is dry enough, throwing sliding three sixties in the black mud. Driving a new art form, an adventure with shovels.

They gallop *en masse* past the homestead to the yards, the drumbeat of seventy times four hooves sounding like the beginning and the end of the world. Makes you hold your breath in deep. The vibration comes first, beating closer, shuddering the very air. Then the blur of them, bay, black, buckskin, grey. Manes and tails flying, shoulder to flank to nose, the grunt of air and effort.

They wheel into the homestead yards. A thousand galahs rise screeching to the sky, gliding and joking their way back to the shade trees as the horses take turns gulping at the trough. Diamonds of water drip from their soft muzzles in the breaking light. Kicking and bucking in protest as, one by one, they are caught. Feet trimmed, tangles pulled from mane and tail, remembered of manners. All the eye rolling and shyness is for show, they rest their chins on our shoulders and whicker impatiently for oats.

The bungarras round the house yard are fat and sleek and shiny. Engorged roo ticks cling to their elbows. They slide from under the house as the morning sun begins to warm the soil, hunting frogs. The dog lifts a lazy eyebrow and goes back to dozing. Around the edges of drying puddles bright yellow butterflies cluster like petals, drinking, drinking. They rise in a golden cloud as I walk the red road toward the workshop, land in my hair, on my arms. They transform me.

Saddles are dragged from shed rafters, wet season mould scraped off. Surcingles oiled, blankets washed and hung in the sharpening evening air. Humidity is still high, night still warm as day and we test each breeze waiting for the desert air to reach us. Waiting for the dragonflies to arrive in mosquito killing squadrons. Bauhinia trees drip honey in our hair.

In the paddocks cattle graze up to their bellies in pasture. Calves are dropping. Beautiful long eared gangly babies racing up to the car with curious liquid eyes, their mothers watching fiercely. The bulls, humps clustered with buffel fly, lie somnolent under the scattered trees. Everything growing, waiting.

Wirralburu Season – May
The Bloodwoods begin to flower. Black cockatoos fly screeching to the tree tops and shred the leaves, destruction in their wake. The puddles are all gone. The first signs of dust rise from our footsteps, powder soft in our toes. Early morning the air hums with slow diving dragonflies. The mosquitoes are gone.

In the clear evenings air travelling east from the interior catches in our throats and we reach for cardigans and flannel shirts tucked away since last September. In the mornings thick sea fog blankets sound, bending it to curious directions, spangling spiderwebs on the fencewire.

We ride out on the floodplains, the jingle of bridles in our ears and the sweet smell of horse. The buffel has seeded and crowns deep purple as far as the eye can see. With the first tentative easterly breezes it ripples like a great inland sea, dipping and folding in on itself. Ground quail rush beneath the horses' hooves and small grass birds fly beside us unafraid, snatching up grasshoppers dislodged by our travels.

Ivory breasted sea eagles fly inward from the coast, wing tips dipped in ink, hunting small lizards scurrying amidst the grasses and up the trunks of trees. Red breasted kites *kee kee* in the cooling air and alight on fenceposts, watching, waiting. Samphire plains out toward the ocean turn amethyst in the late afternoon light, the grey dust roadway glows midnight blue. Dust from our vehicles hangs like an echo in the air behind us when we go out to the coastline crabbing.

In the mangroves the sea clicks through gnarled roots. Here is a turtle sunning in the grey mud. Here the great sliding tracks of a croc. At low tide we walk for miles, dogs and children splashing through the shallow creeks. Always one eye on the seawater moving inwards, the silent turn of tide. Too easy to be cut off by a fast filling creek as water rushes back in on us. Too many near misses to ignore the signs.

Wader birds run on tiptoe away from our progress.

Some years ago, South Korea filled its mangrove flats with concrete for urban housing, the press of humans pushing forward, ever forward over the muddy flatland. These same waders fly from Siberia, a world away, following a course charted by some mysterious ancient longing to feed here on the shores of Roebuck bay. They are small birds; you can hold them in one hand, so tiny to be so brave. Halfway here they would stop to feed, to rest and gather strength for the remainder of their monumental flight. Right there, where the housing is now. Imagine their surprise and dismay, the tired beating of tawny wings as they circle familiar ground now changed beyond understanding to make way for more of *us*. Imagine them flying onward with grim resignation. Weaker birds falling from sky to ocean, less making it here every year.

Down at the yards we oil the gates and crush, ready for the work ahead, strengthen any weaker top rails. Restart the pumps as the cattle move back onto water. Grease the windmills and wipe clean the solar panels. Service the vehicles. Shake the frogshit, dry and shiny with insect wings, out of our workboots. The agents arrive, one by one, checking the cattle in the paddocks with a practised eye. Forward contracts are signed, handshakes all round. Endless cups of tea on the shady verandas and out under the Tamarind tree. A breathless hope that the season goes well. That no one is injured. That prices stay strong.

We curse the bungarras in a fond tones as they burrow deep ready for the winter. In the newly dug vegetable garden, in the middle of the path to the clothesline, under the schoolroom floor. Reptilian eyes pass over us unconcerned as they soak up the last warmth of the flagstones.

Barrgana Season – June to August

Winter blows in with an easterly desert chill. Electricity snaps from our hair, our hands, the car door. Hands and lips are chapped and sore. Up in the icy dark before dawn; saddle the horse with leather hard and stiff. Ride out the first snort and buck of the day and settle into a rhythm. The leather warms and softens to shape though we both, man and horse, blow white smoke with our breath like dragons. We muster down by the mill where the sergeant was speared all those years ago. 1864. We ride in there through a tunnel of tea tree. It's dark and quiet. The horses are spooked by the hollow sound of their hooves over the underground streams. No one lingers, no one camps there. I imagine them asleep by campfires as, through the trees shadow men glide. It's been cattle country for a long time around here, in our timeframe anyway, but it's never been a comfortable ride. There's been a lot of looking the other way.

Long days follow in the sandy yards, drafting cattle; weaners, branders, wets, drys, culls, heifers, breeders, bulls. Black dust rises in the dry air and we cough soil and cowshit up all night, clearing our throats. After dinner and on into the night the separated weaners call for their mothers and their mothers call back. In the liquid spill of moonlight, we walk down to the holding yards to check on the cattle. They are restless. There are wild dogs about, we can hear them calling, followed by the high *yip yip* of the pups; learning to hunt. A shiver sound in the dark. Our own dogs slink under the house, ears flat, feigning sleep.

In the dawn light road trains pull in, six deckers, the driver always ready for a cup of tea and a yarn. He's been all over, carries the gossip with him. We ease the steers up the race and onto the truck, they're quiet, hardly woken. Twenty five to a deck, six times each truck. Gates clang and slam. The truckie walks the metal path along the top deck checking the load is even, too high for me, he's easy up there. As the trucks pull out we watch them go. The steers turn and look at us, noses poked through the rails. Breaks your heart all over again. Its eerie quiet then, the yards empty, hay scattered over the ground knee deep. We spend a while there picking up the bailing twine and talking softly. It's melancholy. Whatever your politics, it takes more than you think to sell your friends.

Town is full of tourists but we go there anyway, to celebrate the job done, to distract ourselves. It's overbright there and noisy. We don't stay long.

Wirlburu season – September

Night loses its chill. During the day temperatures begin to soar into the mid-forties, a sea breeze late in the day a welcome relief. Some days are too hot to work cattle, both for them and us, too hot to ride. Time is spent catching up on all the things we have let slide in the flurry of mustering. Schoolbooks are reopened to the kids' dismay. Spelling rules and maths no match for the previous excitement. No one's very enthusiastic. The teachers come out to visit and wilt without air conditioning but the kids are keen as anything to see them and have the day planned out for sport and science and art. The things we don't get time for left to our own devices.

A German backpacker turns up on a bicycle, half dead from thirst and the heat. Drinks gallons of cordial. He's hopelessly lost, lucky to have found us out here. Stays six weeks repairing fencelines, having the time of his life and leaves only reluctantly as his visa runs out. At night we go out with firestarters to backburn on the road verges if the Westerly is strong enough to be safe. Hoping to get enough cool burns in to slow the wildfires we know will come with the build up to the wet.

There's a mining company scouting around the place. Driving around in landcruisers looking for gas, diamonds, kaolin, anything of value they can find. They resent having to ask about the road conditions and directions to the more remote areas of the station. We resent everything they stand for. Where we see beauty they see dongas in regimented rows and drillers and dollars. There's no common ground. Never will be.

The wader birds fly past in brown battalions heading for Siberia again. Our hearts go with them, wishing them Godspeed.

Laja season – October November

Build up time. The humidity becomes a blanket, sucking all the oxygen out of the air. It's still dry, rain is a long way off. The grasses are sparse and grey under the blaze of an unforgiving sun. Smoke haze hangs about in the still mornings. The Kimberley is on fire again. The death toll amongst wildlife is frightening. Birds drop dead from the yellowed sky or sit drooped under the sprinklers. Beaks gasped open, wings outstretched. One fire is started by a tourist pulling his Porsche over on the highway verge to take a piss and leaving the engine running in the tinder grass. Hundreds, thousands of hectares burn.

Bungarras start to appear again, coming out from their hibernation along with numerous snakes. They're all thin as sticks and hungry as hell, cranky too. Like everyone else they're waiting, waiting for the wet. The night sky is lit by distant desert lightning storms. Beautiful to watch but it just means more fires and we watch for smoke continually. The acacias split their pods all over the ground, native bees fill their nests with honey from the flowering sandalwood trees.

The Yawuru custodians go stingray fishing out on the coast. It's the last chance before the wet makes all the roads out that way impassable in a bottomless swill of black mud. The women come for ceremony out across the wide plain to their own places. They come every year. Have been forever. Before the pieces of paper, before the horses, before us. One of the older ladies stands by the Tamarind tree, declines to come in the house. No, she says, half blind with glaucoma and leaning on a stick. I wonder what she really thinks of us, how much forgiveness she is able to find, how much of her silence is protest. She is keen to get out to women's country, relieved to get back in the car amongst the teenagers, the angry daughter. They stop again on their way out and she stays in the car, now smiling, renewed. Every year she is shading to frail and coming out here is harder on her. She's on dialysis now. I wonder who will hold her power when she is gone.

Out on the plain the brolgas are back in the afternoons, dancing with the sunset sky as a backdrop.

Man-gala season – December to March

The first rains fall. Great sweeping storms wash in from the coast, thunderheads brilliant white with the sunlight still behind them. Thunder shakes through our feet and rattles the house walls. Calves and foals, born in the dry, run recklessly through the skidding mud, amazed at how their world has transformed. The rain is too loud on the roof to talk, it numbs our ears, makes a mockery of trying to listen to the news. Who's had rain and how much?

Frogs call from the rafters in competition and a python follows their vibrations up the window frame. Life is suddenly, shockingly, a raucous riot of slitherings and chatterings and booming rolls of ozone. Everything bursts into life at once. The lizards are sleek again, snakes thicker than your arm. Mosquitoes breed in the millions and out on the plains, where weeks ago we were mustering, there is a great shining lake knee deep in swarming thick bodied tadpoles.

We wake to the sound of Ibis and wild ducks feeding on the lawn. Wallabies thump and cough in the night, carousing at all hours. Poinciana trees around the homestead blaze crimson and frangipani scents the steamy air. Everything is always damp, everything grows mould. The rain is a renewal of everything around us, all the burnt places spring up new green growth. Instead of fires we watch for cyclones, those howling screaming banshee nights when our frailty is thrown in our faces, watch anxiously as they peel off down the coast.

Three months into the wet and all we can think about is the dry. Tired of the rain, tired of the humidity. Ready for work to begin again.

Season's end

When the time came to leave that place I had two years to say goodbye and yet I never could say the words. The idea of being *away* left me shipwrecked. All my years there a pebble thrown in a still pond, a scant ripple and then calm, as though it never was. For me, living on and beginning to understand the country had caused a seismic shift toward what was true and clear in life and I would never be the same.

That country grew me up, taught me what was important to know. I know where and when the turtles nest out on that coast but I don't have to go and see for myself. It is enough to know they are there. They don't need my footprints on their sand or my camera in their tired patient faces. The earth doesn't need my sticky fingerprints all over everything.

I know there are dinosaur footprints out there in the rock on the coastline. I know there are secret places, sacred places, where I do not need to go to make them special. I know that ultimately the kindest type of environmentalism is learning to leave things alone, to be silent about the special things and have the humility not to speak of them to others. I know the land endures. The land endures *us*. The land just is. Therein lies our comfort.

They say, the old people, the country gets into your blood. It's more than that. At the same time your skin is seeping salt and sweat, your lungs are drawing in the dust of the place. It settles somewhere deep and gathers there until you are still partly you, yet partly country too. The lines begin to blur between who you were and what you are. When I die how much of the dust I become will be desert dust? How much of who I am is made up of where I was?

On our last school camp for remote students to the city, heavy with the knowledge I would soon need to relearn how to live in such a crowded, noisy place, I was given charge of five young indigenous girls from a community further north. Their home was even more far flung than ours, accessible over the rugged range country only by light aircraft. The big city was a revelation to them. As we walked through the amazement and thrill of a theme park they shone with the wonder of modern miracles and mechanics. Skipped and laughed and ran and peppered me with questions.

'Where you from?' They asked me.

'Oh, I don't know. All about.'

'Where your people are?'

'All over the place I guess,' I said, that old familiar feeling creeping over me. 'Not anywhere particular.'

'Where's your country then?' They were exasperated at my obtuse answers. Believing I was joking because my truth was, to them, simply inconceivable.

It was difficult talking around the sudden lump in my throat. 'I don't have country.'

'Oh.' They paused, looking at each other wide eyed. Girls who had nothing much material, who ate mostly by campfires and lived out bush, who read their country like a bible. Read it through their eyes and hearts, their very breath. They slid long warm fingers firm around my own, leant in to me with their sharp shoulders, liquid eyes full of pity. 'No country? Big shame.'

THE NIGHT GRANDMA TURNED INTO A GOAT

by Maureen O'Keefe

This story belongs to my uncles. Alfie Jungarrayi Brown and Joe Jungarrayi Murphy and is about their father who lived with his wife in a beautiful spot next to a hot spring just east of McClaren Creek. Uncle Joe told the story to my cousin Mary Louise Murphy and she passed it on to me.

One evening my grandparents were sitting outside their humpy, telling stories with their son, my uncle. They were having a family gathering, like Aboriginal people still do today, and enjoying themselves when a big rain came.

'Come on Nakamara, let's go inside because it's starting to rain now,' grandpa said to grandma. And off they went into their humpy. Made out of spinifex grass, twigs and leaves, it looked like an upside down nest. There was no bed inside, just a blanket on the ground. But they were happy in their little humpy and soon both of them were fast asleep, their backs against each other.

Sometime during the night grandpa rolled over on his side and put his hand out in the dark to feel if grandma was still there, sleeping beside him.

'Oh there you are Nakamarra,' he said, touching her shoulder softly. He was happy his wife was there, sleeping right beside him. But as he rubbed grandmother's shoulder a little more, he felt something strange.

'Hey Nakamarra,' he said in a sleepy voice, 'how come you've grown so much hair in the night?' But there was no reply. All he could hear was the sound of the rain.

Grandpa then moved his hands upwards to feel for his wife's face, his fingers gently resting on her chin. He wanted to make sure it was his wife lying there beside him and not a dream. Once again, he felt something strange.

'Hey Nakamarra, how come you grown a beard too?' Grandpa was still half asleep, and he couldn't understand why grandma had suddenly got so hairy in the middle of the night. It was dark too. And since it was so dark he couldn't see who was beside him. So he touched the top of what he thought was grandma's head. This time he felt something really strange.

'Hey Nakamarra, how come you've grown two horns as well?' On the other side of the blanket grandma could hear grandpa talking to someone. She had moved to where it was dry in the night to get away from the dripping rain.

'Japaljarri,' she said to the old man in language, 'who are you talking to?'

Well, that's when that old man opened his eyes. His mind bin sleepy before but when he realised his wife was not there on the bed lying next to him he suddenly woke up.

'Hey Nakamarra, how come you are over there on the other side of the bed?' he asked.

'Rain bin dripping on me. I moved to where it's dry,' she replied.

'Then who am I talking to?' he asked. 'And who is this big hairy person lying next to me?' Grandma didn't know. It was too dark to see. Grandpa called out to his son.

'Jungarrayi, Jungarrayi, come quick, and bring a torch.' My uncle heard his father call out to him. He was worried for that old man, wondering why he needed a torch so urgently in the middle of the night, and ran to his humpy quickly. When uncle reached the humpy, grandpa grabbed the torch and shone the light at the strange figure lying beside him.

'I want to see who's sleeping in my bed,' he told his wife. Well, didn't he get the biggest shock of his life. Sleeping on its side, right next to him, was one of grandpa's billy goats. He was quite comfortable there, lying on the blankets and out of the rain.

'Aya,aya,' yelled grandpa. 'I thought it was you Nakamarra. I didn't know I was talking to a goat.'

Grandma and uncle both laughed when they heard that. They laughed so much, there were tears in their eyes. But grandpa was really angry. He was so mad at that goat he whacked it on the head with the torch and booted him out of the humpy. Poor old billy goat had to sleep out in the rain that night. But you know what it never tried to sneak into the humpy again and grandpa never mistook grandma for a goat again either.

ULURU STATEMENT FROM THE HEART

We, gathered at the 2017 National Constitutional Convention, coming from all points of the southern sky, make this statement from the heart:

Our Aboriginal and Torres Strait Islander tribes were the first sovereign Nations of the Australian continent and its adjacent islands and possessed it under our own laws and customs. This our ancestors did, according to the reckoning of our culture, from the Creation, according to the common law from 'time immemorial', and according to science more than 60,000 years ago.

This sovereignty is a *spiritual notion: the ancestral tie between the land, or 'mother nature', and the Aboriginal and Torres Strait Islander peoples who were born therefrom, remain attached thereto, and must one day return thither to be united with our ancestors. This link is the basis of the ownership of the soil, or better, of sovereignty*. It has never been ceded or extinguished and co-exists with the sovereignty of the Crown.

How could it be otherwise? That peoples possessed a land for sixty millennia and this sacred link disappears from world history in merely the last two hundred years?

With substantive constitutional change and structural reform, we believe this ancient sovereignty can shine through as a fuller expression of Australia's nationhood.

Proportionally, we are the most incarcerated people on the planet. We are not an innately criminal people. Our children are aliened from their families at unprecedented rates. This cannot be because we have no love for them. And our youth languish in detention in obscene numbers. They should be our hope for the future.

These dimensions of our crisis tell plainly the structural nature of our problem. This is *the torment of our powerlessness*.

We seek constitutional reforms to empower our people and take a *rightful place* in our own country. When we have power over our destiny our children will flourish. They will walk in two worlds and their culture will be a gift to their country.

We call for the establishment of a First Nations Voice enshrined in the Constitution.

Makarrata is the culmination of our agenda: *the coming together after a struggle*. It captures our aspirations for a fair and truthful relationship with the people of Australia and a better future for our children based on justice and self-determination.

We seek a Makarrata Commission to supervise a process of agreement-making between governments and First Nations and truth-telling about our history.

In 1967 we were counted, in 2017 we seek to be heard. We leave base camp and start our trek across this vast country. We invite you to walk with us in a movement of the Australian people for a better future.

AUTHOR BIOGRAPHIES

Marie Munkara Born on the banks of the Mainoru River Marie Munkara spent her early years on Bathurst Island. Her first book *Every Secret* thing won the David Unaipon Award in 2008 and the NT Book of the Year in 2010 and she has written a second novel *A Most Peculiar Act*. She has also written two children's books *Rusty Brown* and *Rusty and Jojo* Her memoir *Of Ashes and Rivers that Run to the Sea* was shortlisted for the NSW Premiers Award 2017 and is currently being made into a film. Her sixth book is scheduled for publication in 2021.

Merlinda Bobis has had four novels, six poetry books, and a collection of short stories published, and ten dramatic works performed. Her novel *Locust Girl*, *A Lovesong* received the Christina Stead Prize for Fiction in the NSW Premier's Literary Awards and the Philippine National Book Award. Her poetry collection *Accidents of Composition* was Highly Commended for the ACT Book of the Year Award. For her, writing is homecoming: a return to roots, a retrieval through memory, and a reckoning with loss, hopefully with care and grace. She lives and writes in Ngunnawal Country (Canberra).

Rachel Bin Salleh is descended from the Nimunburr and Yawuru peoples of the Kimberley. Rachel is the publisher at Magabala Books and is passionate about First Nations peoples telling their stories. Rachel wrote her first book *Alfred's War* (2018).

Claire Aman lives in Grafton, NSW. She worked as roadhouse cook, barmaid, storeman and then environmental planner, writing on the side. Her short story collection *Bird Country* was published in 2017. Her stories have won the E J Brady, Wet Ink, David Harold Tribe and Hal Porter prizes. Her work has appeared in Australian Short Stories, Griffith Review, Heat, Southerly, Best Australian Stories, Australian Book Review and Island magazine. She is a co-founder of the Long Way Home community writing project in the Clarence Valley.

Alan Jackson is a Mooriwarri man and is a descendant of the Hospital Creek massacre. He asked us to record his story in 2020 as he is anxious that the old stories are preserved.

Brad Steadman born and bred and most likely will be buried in Brewarrina so this is my main ancestral life experience wahwangiya as and through mimibah which also extends and includes gangarahmakay and barrinahtji as bungkal widi through and as garigabah. The above use of relationship names such as mimibah and garigabah as maeingalgahdei my mob and landed names such as wahwangiya gangarahmakay is an attempt to explain without getting too complicated or simplistic but to go beyond the limited enforced authoritarian vocabulary of tribe or nation as a more land expansive and interrelated land people place.

Dianne Kelly lives at Brewarrina. She has been immersed in her culture for a long time and is keen to begin telling her stories. Bruce Pascoe met her at the Clontarf unit at the Brewarrina school.

Jim Berg is a Gunditjmara Elder

Tony Birch is the author of three novels: the bestselling *The White Girl*, winner of the 2020 NSW Premier's Award for Indigenous Writing; *Ghost River*, winner of the 2016 Victorian Premier's Literary Award for Indigenous Writing; and *Blood*, which was shortlisted for the Miles Franklin Award. He is also the author of *Shadowboxing* and three short story collections, *Father's Day, The Promise and Common People*. In 2017 he was awarded the Patrick White Literary Award. Tony is a frequent contributor to ABC local and national radio, a regular guest at writers' festivals, and a climate justice campaigner. He lives in Melbourne.

David Whish-Wilson is the author of seven novels and three non-fiction books, including the four novels in the Frank Swann crime series and the Perth book in the NewSouth city series. He also writes short fiction, essays and reviews. David's next novel is The Sawdust House, out with Fremantle Press in 2022. He lives with his wife and three kids in Fremantle, WA.

Julia Prendergast lives in Melbourne with her circus of a family. Julia's short stories have been longlisted, shortlisted and published: Lightship Anthology 2 (UK), Glimmer Train (US), TEXT (AU) Séan Ó Faoláin Competition, (IE), Review of Australian Fiction, Australian

Book Review Elizabeth Jolley Prize, Josephine Ulrick Prize (AU). Julia's novel is forthcoming with the University of Western Australia Press (UWAP). Julia has a PhD in Writing and Literature. She is a lecturer in Writing and Literature at Swinburne University in Melbourne (AU).

Melissa Lucashenko is a Goorie author of Bundjalung and European heritage. Her first novel, *Steam Pigs*, was published in 1997 and since then her work has received acclaim in many literary awards. *Too Much Lip* is her sixth novel and won the 2019 Miles Franklin Literary Award and the Queensland Premier's Award for a Work of State Significance. It was also shortlisted for the Prime Minister's Literary Award for Fiction, the Stella Prize, two Victorian Premier's Literary Awards, two Queensland Literary Awards and two NSW Premier's Literary Awards. Melissa is a Walkley Award winner for her non-fiction, and a founding member of human rights organisation Sisters Inside. She writes about ordinary Australians and the extraordinary lives they lead.

Ian Hood and **Roger Vickery** have been friends and collaborators since their high school days in Albury.

Ian is a painter and writer who has spent much of his life travelling. He now lives near Bermagui on the NSW South Coast. In 2017 he won the Thunderbolt Crime Poetry Award. That poem, like *Ragtime in Eden*, was inspired by journals he kept while working on fishing boats.

Roger lives in Sydney. He has won more than 70 writing awards for poetry, fiction, plays and scripts. His work has been published in Australia and overseas. Two co-written plays (about refugees on the run and Afghanistan war veterans, respectively) recently enjoyed very successful productions. He is co-writing a TV crime/terrorism series set in 'post-Christchurch Australia'.

Graham Sheil: Born Melbourne 1938, left school at 15 to work in optical workshops and has worked since in wholesale optics. In 1972 founded the company that became Australia's major supplier of magnification for rehabilitation of the visually impaired and has extensively lectured. Over a hundred short stories published, two collections of stories, a novel and plays performed. *This Is The Way The World Ends* was shortlisted for the (Victorian) Premiers Award for drama, and *Bali: Adat* was performed by Melbourne Theatre Company for the Melbourne Festival of Arts. At present working on two novels, a novella and more stories.

Leslie Thiele is a writer based in the south west of Western Australia. Her short fiction centres around her characters reactions to the world they live in and social change. A keen student of human nature in all its manifestations, Leslie drops people into imagined situations and environments and waits to see what they will do. Recently completing her Bachelor of Arts in creative writing and literature at Edith Cowan University's regional campus in Bunbury has further refined her writing and led to her gaining recognition for pieces of her work in various competitions, events and spoken performances. Leslie's collection of short fiction, *Skyglow*, was published by Margaret River Press in 2020.

Maureen Jipyiliya Nampijimpa O'Keefe is an artist, writer, artefact maker, storyteller, storykeeper translator and interpreter. Her family comes from the Devil's Marbles area also known as Karlu Karlu, and she is a Kaytetye-Warlpiri woman born and raised in Ali-Curung, south-east of Tennant Creek. Maureen's short stories and poems appear in *This Country Anytime Anywhere* (IAD Press 2010), Desert Writing (UWA Publishing 2016), ABC Online and in the Red Room's *The Disappearing* App. In 2014 she was the recipient of the Magabala Books Australian Indigenous Creators' Scholarship and she has performed at Writers' Festivals across the country.